Murder in Christmas River

A Christmas Cozy Mystery

Book 1

Meg Muldoon

Vacant Lot Publishing

Meg Muldoon Books
207 Sugar Pine Drive
Bend, Oregon
www.megmuldoon.com

Publisher's Note: This is a work of fiction. Names, characters, places, and incidents are a product of the author's imagination. Locales and public names are sometimes used for atmospheric purposes. Any resemblance to actual people, living or dead, or to businesses, companies, events, institutions, or locales is completely coincidental.

Murder in Christmas River/ Meg Muldoon. — 1st ed.
ISBN 978198036438-2

To M & P
For always being there

PROLOGUE

He went back to the scene of it all, deep into the woods, the place where his journey had started.

The dog hadn't liked the tone of the woman's voice. There was something desperate in it. Something shrill and bad. Something ominous.

His hair bristled. He felt like growling, lifting his lips and revealing his sharp teeth, but he knew it would only be met by a scold and some yelling from his owner.

This was an odd place they were in. The dog had been here before, but each time, it felt new and strange. The ground was cold against his paws, and white pieces of cold fell from the sky sometimes, getting in his eyes and making his fur damp and heavy.

The dog was used to warmer weather.

His master raised his voice, his thunderous sound echoing against the trees in the woods. The dog dug his claws into the snow. Sounds he couldn't understand came out of his owner's mouth.

Then, there was movement. Fast movement. The dog readied for attack. His owner grabbed the woman's arm. There was a struggle. The dog lunged for the woman's leg. She screamed out.

There was the sound of steel going into flesh. The dog dug his teeth deeper into the leg, tasting blood and salt.

His master crumpled to the ground, a coppery smell filling the air.

The dog felt a stiff kick to his rib cage that sent him flying back. The woman ran. The dog ran after her, nipping at her heels. She carried his owner's smell with her.

But then she reached a car, and the dog could only bark at her, growling as the car backed up and peeled away from the trail parking lot.

The dog didn't have to go back into the woods to know his owner was dead.

But he did.

He stood over him as white flakes fell from the sky and clung to his owner's lifeless body.

He watched as it accumulated. He barked, but his cries were muffled and carried away by the sharp winds.

No one else came.

The dog was alone.

CHAPTER 1

I'm not sentimental.

I'm not sappy or soft or gooey. In the spring when Girl Scouts come to my business looking to sell me some overpriced thin mints, I send them packing. In the fall when all the ladies of Christmas River start planning the annual Christmas parade, I can be found back at my pie shop, working hard on getting the seasonal Christmas Pie just right. That, or I can be found drinking down at the Pine Needle Tavern with two old-timers who like to recount the glory days of Christmas River before the lumber mill shut down.

During the annual Christmas River Gingerbread Junction Competition held every year the second week of December, I take no prisoners. I aim to kill, and I shoot to win.

That's me. My name is Cinnamon, and my mom had some foresight on her when she named me that.

She knew that I had a kick to me.

No. Sentimental isn't normally something I identify with.

But something about that dog out there, with his matted

fur all thick with snowflakes, and the way he's shivering and shaking in that cutting Central Oregon Cascade mountains kind-of-wind, and the way that he bolts every time I so much as go for the door knob, and the fear and sadness in his little eyes… looking like somebody did something bad to him. Looking like the way I did about two years ago.

Something about him has turned me into a big bowl of hot pie filling, oozing and bubbling over the sides of the pan. All melted and gooey and sweet.

Jeez, I've even got a name I'm calling him now: Huckleberry.

I watched him as he slopped away noisily at the almost empty tin pie pan while keeping his fearful eyes glued on me. He couldn't even really enjoy the leftover pie like that, ready to jump if I so much moved from my statue-like stance at the backdoor window.

The snow was coming down in heavy flakes, standing out against the dog's black fur. It probably had been lustrous at one point, the way Australian Shepherd's fur usually is. Now it was all matted and muddy. Tear stains clung to the corners of his sad little eyes, a desperation of hunger in them.

He had a thin red collar around his neck, but no tag.

I hated thinking how his little stomach must have grumbled.

He could have been a poster dog for one of those humane society commercials, with words at the bottom of the screen saying something like, *when will my next meal be?*

Poor thing.

This was the third time this week he'd come to the back porch of my pie shop. He came out of the woods that bordered the back of my store. I didn't know if it was the bright lights shining through the black night that brought him, or the smell of late-night pastries and the promise of scraps. But for whatever reason, he'd show up on my back porch.

When it first happened, I opened the door and tried to lure him inside with some leftover Marionberry pie. He took off back into the woods, but an hour later, he was right back there, shivering on the steps.

I finally left a pie tin of scraps on the porch for him to eat in his own good time. And as I watched him nervously devour the leftovers, I gave him a name. Huckleberry. It really should have been Marionberry, but that sounded too much like a girl's name. The dog was a boy dog, and needed a stronger name.

Huckleberry.

The next morning, I called the sheriff's office about the stray. But either nobody had any luck catching him, or catching a lost dog wasn't high on anybody's priority list.

Since then, he'd visited the back porch a couple more times. Each time late at night. Each time, when nobody could catch him. Each time, I'd leave a tin of the day's leftover pie for him. Each night, I'd watch him eat, and he'd watch me.

I wanted to help him more, but he wouldn't let me.

I looked out the window and fought off a chill that traveled up my spine. A bitter winter's chill that had stayed with me for the past two years. Sometimes it would just strike me out of nowhere. In the height of a summer day, I'd be hit with a bout of shivers. My body would go numb, and it was like I'd get caught in a thick fog for a while.

I never had the chills up until two years ago.

Huckleberry suddenly stopped slopping at the tin. His ears pricked up, and his hair bristled, and within a split second, he was gone.

I watched him run back into the woods, disappearing into the darkness.

I stared out into those black, frozen woods as the chills overpowered me.

I wasn't sentimental. But that didn't mean I didn't sometimes fall back into my own memories on dark, vacuous nights like tonight.

Me and Huckleberry. Each in our own darkness.

I didn't feel warm again until the next morning.

CHAPTER 2

Christmas River: Where the Christmas Spirit Never Dies.

That's on the cheerful welcome sign when you drive through Christmas River. Beneath it, it lists the population: 5,030.

It doesn't say the truth, which is that the town died a long time ago. The real town, at least.

The town was named after the crystal clean river it was built around. But when the lumber mill shut down 30 years ago, things changed. A lot. Christmas ornament shops suddenly started springing up. Gift shops and coffee huts and art galleries weren't far behind. They put in an ice rink in the lumber mill parking lot. In a scramble to keep from dying, the town milked its name for all it was worth. Soon, Christmas River wasn't just a town to drive through: it became a primary pit stop. A destination that people across the state would come to for a little bit of manufactured Christmas cheer year round.

I'm 33, but I know what the town once was. My grandfather has enough stories in him about the way things used to be to write a book the size of *War and Peace*. He talks about the way Christmas River used to be populated by blue-collar workers, working hard to support their families and make ends meet. Good people. Not the casual, spoiled tourists that now outweighed the real residents most days of the year.

My hometown has become a novelty. A place of forced smiles and customer satisfaction. Of little old ladies dressing up as Mrs. Claus and trying to sell you something. Of capitalizing and merchandising the magic of the season year round.

My grandfather says it's practically unrecognizable these days.

But what's bad is what's good sometimes. The trees aren't complaining, and I'm not either. The town's reinvented façade is part of the reason why my pie shop, *Cinnamon's Pies*, has done so well. It's a lot of the reason why I can live back here and help take care of my grandfather.

Plus, I'm not all gloom and doom when it comes to Christmas. I do enjoy some things about the holiday.

Like perfecting my seasonal edition of Cinnamon's Christmas Pie, or helping my neighbor's kids build their first snow fort of the season, or lighting candles in windows during December blizzards.

Or the annual Christmas River Gingerbread Junction Competition held the second week of December every year.

Especially the Gingerbread Junction Competition.

The grand prize is a four-day trip to Maui.

But it's not even about the trip to Maui. There's much more at stake than tropical palm trees, warm waters and Mai Tai cocktails.

It's about the title. To be known as the Junction queen. To be recognized as more creative, crafty and clever than anybody else that year.

I started participating in the competition when I was 15. When I was 17, I got my first win. There were a few years I missed while I was away at college, but ever since I was 23, I've been in every single gingerbread house competition.

That's 10 years of straight competitions.

Every year, people come from all over the Northwest come to ogle the gingerbread art we create. Some of the competitors spend all year preparing for it, creating blueprint after blueprint for epic cookie houses with intricate decorations. For some of us, it becomes an obsession.

Or maybe that's just me.

The past two years, I've become particularly obsessed with creating the grandest gingerbread house the world has ever seen.

I've won five competitions altogether, and come in second place most of the other times, except for two years ago, when I bombed out of the competition completely. It ended in a week-long depression-driven pie binge where each night I'd go home, drink glass after glass of white wine and eat leftover pie and sob while watching late-night soul music infomercials.

There were obviously other reasons for my meltdown. But the loss and utter humiliation of not even placing in the competition really killed me.

But I was determined to redeem myself from that experience. This year, I was determined to show everyone that I was back. I wanted to show them that I couldn't be beaten so easily. That I wasn't a has-been. That I could still create works of art through sugar, flour, and spices.

I had to prove to them that I was a winner.

If only my gingerbread house building partner was as focused.

"Next thing I knew, he was looking at me with this absolutely horrified expression on his face. I can't even describe it, Cin. The kind of pain the man must have been in. I mean, the coffee spilled all over him," she said. "And the most horrible thing about it all was that for some reason, I just wanted to start giggling. I mean, I just had the worst time containing myself."

Kara's face broke out into a smile, revealing two perfectly straight rows of perfect white teeth.

I shook my head, hunching over the first story of the gingerbread mansion we were working on.

"I can't believe you," I said.

"I know, I can't believe myself either sometimes," she said. She was still smiling. "There *oughta* be a law against me."

We were in the back of the pie shop. It was late afternoon— a time of the day that rarely saw visitors. We were in the kitchen, working on the first step in the week-long process of building an elaborate, award-winning gingerbread house.

Well, at least one of us was working. Kara was talking more shop than slaving away, but that was okay. It was going to be a long evening.

Kara had been my best friend since high school. She was a platinum blonde who, true to her hair color, had a lot of spark and tenacity. She was loud and abrasive, and acted like a bull in a china shop sometimes. But despite her general noisiness, Kara had a deep love for crafting and was a hard worker. Her store, *Ornate Ornaments*, did well, especially during the winter and summer tourist seasons. People would buy ornaments in Christmas River even when it wasn't Christmas.

She was a smart business woman.

Even though we'd been best friends for a long time, it wasn't always that way. When I moved away from Christmas River to go to college, we lost touch. It wasn't until I moved back five years ago to take care of my grandpa and set up shop that we started talking again.

I never completely understood why Kara had never left Central Oregon. She always seemed like she was made for a big city, but Kara had never gotten much farther than Farewell, a town 30 minutes west that was about three times the size of Christmas River. She had met and married a man out there, and moved there for him. But four years into the marriage, things fell apart. And when they did, Kara came back home to this side of the mountains, and opened up her ornament shop.

We were similar in that way. We both knew what it was like to have the rug ripped out from underneath us. To have it all fall apart.

"Well, are you going to see him again?" I asked. "Or are you going to let the poor man die of shame?"

Since her divorce, Kara had been going through what seemed like hundreds of dates. She must have dated just about every eligible bachelor in Christmas River and the surrounding towns.

Nothing ever seemed to work out, though. But her dates did always make for good stories.

Part of me wondered if Kara wasn't just going through the motions of it, and that she was still hung up on her ex. She was likeable enough, and despite what she wanted it to seem like sometimes, she did have heart. She was pretty, too. Kara could easily have had just about any of those eligible bachelors if she really wanted to.

"I seriously don't know if I'll get that image out of my head," she said. "I mean, I can try, but I just know, knowin' me, that sometime he'll be talking to me about something serious, and it's going to pop back in my head and I'll start laughing."

I shook my head again disapprovingly.

"You can't build a relationship with that kind of starting point, can you?" she continued. "Sometimes you just have to quit while you're ahead, you know what I mean?"

"But what if he's a really nice guy?" I asked while gluing together the walls of the main floor grand entrance with powdered sugar frosting. "What if he's your soul mate and he had one bad moment where he lost his grip on his mug? You can't hold that against him, can you?"

"All's fair in love and war, which includes dropping a guy because he spilled coffee all over himself on your first date," Kara said, shrugging. "Anyway, I've stopped believing in soul mates. Mine's been way overdue for too long. I'm beginning to think he's forgotten about me."

Kara tossed a used-up pastry bag into the trash can, like she was tossing out Craig Canby's hopes at a second date with her as well.

"Don't give me that look Cinnamon," she said, catching my gaze at the sad pastry bag in the trash can. "I'm not as heartless as all that, and you know it. But sadly, we can't all find doctors to ride off into the sunset with like you."

I let out a long sigh and looked up at her.

"Let's not go there," I said. "I've got enough on my mind as is."

"You never want to go there," she said. "And I'm your best friend. If you can't talk about it with me, than with who?"

"There's nothing to talk about," I said. "We're just friends."

Kara gave me a look. One of those looks I'd become familiar with in our many years of being friends.

The kind of *I smell bull crap and I'm calling you on it* look.

"You're dead wrong," I said.

"Well, he goes to your pie shop for lunch every afternoon," she said. "I've got enough sense in that department to know that he's not just being friendly."

I started building the support beams of the second floor, feeling like the kitchen was getting stuffy.

"What can I say?" I said. "I make a mean pie. I've got a lot of repeat customers."

"Get out of town," Kara said, rolling her eyes. "As good as the pie is, you know that ain't it."

I suddenly wanted to change the subject.

Mostly, because whenever Kara tried to talk about Dr. John Billings with me, I'd be struck by this wave of confusion mixed in with a little guilt.

John first started coming into the shop about a year ago. Soon, he was there every afternoon at exactly noon. Every day, he'd order a slice of the strawberry rhubarb pie, but he'd never finish the slice. After a few months, I started putting together the fact that John didn't really like pie, and that there were other reasons he was there.

He wasn't a bad sort. He was in his early 40s and had once been married a long time ago, but was now divorced. He moved to Christmas River about five years earlier from Boise to start up his own podiatrist practice. He was smart and good-looking by most standards, and he did a lot of pro-bono work in the community.

Like I said, he wasn't a bad sort.

But sometimes, you just know when something isn't going to work out. I wasn't right for him. I felt it in my bones.

And he wasn't right for me.

But sometimes, I wondered if I was approaching the situation with a closed mind. I was getting older. That was a fact. Plus, he was a nice man. That kind of love that they always talk about, the one that sweeps you off your feet and makes you feel drunk and dizzy and obsessed all the time, I'd been there before. I'd known a love like that before.

And I knew that those kinds of love only ever ended badly. I knew what kind of a monster love like that could turn you into.

Sometimes I wondered if maybe someone like John was just who I needed. Someone who was steadier and calmer. Someone who I could grow to love, maybe. Maybe that's what mature love was. Maybe that was the kind of love that really lasted forever.

I was undecided about John. And in the meantime, it just felt like I was leading him on. He sat there, ordering slice after slice of pie that he didn't even like, while I just took his money and made it seem like he had a chance with me.

"I guess we're not as young as we used to be," Kara said, echoing my own thoughts. "No more Billy Sanders or Kevin Rhines or Daniel Brightmans to serenade us these days. It's not like high school anymore."

I laughed, remembering those three boys from high school. But soon felt a wave of chills run up and down my back.

I didn't like to think about getting older any more than she did. But we weren't *that* old.

"You make it sound like we're fossils," I said.

She sighed.

"Well, lately I've been feeling like one," she said. "Living in a small town doesn't help any."

A shadow passed over her face.

"C'mon," I said, refilling a pastry bag with more frosting sealant. "Fossils wouldn't be able to take Gretchen O'Malley to the floor the way we're going to this weekend, so cheer up."

That made her laugh.

Gretchen O'Malley was our Gingerbread competition

archnemesis. She was a retired, unpleasant woman who was the reigning queen of the competition. I couldn't prove it, but I was pretty sure that when she wasn't scaring children or collecting toadstools and dead ravens for a potion, she spent all her time in the kitchen, working on her gingerbread house.

Gretchen was good at the competition. But we were going to be better this year.

"You're right," she said. "We're going to make her wish that she never picked up a spatula."

I smiled. The bell on the front door jingled, and I put down the pastry bag to go help the late afternoon customer.

Kara smiled as I walked away, but I had a feeling it didn't last too long.

It was hard getting older. It was hard being single and getting older.

It was something I didn't like to think about when I could avoid it.

CHAPTER 3

After I closed the pie shop, I walked on over to the Pine Needle Tavern. The streets had been icy the night before, but now a fine dust of snow settled over the concrete and asphalt.

I passed Gretchen O'Malley by coincidence as I walked there. She was strolling down the street, wearing some sort of fur jacket with giant gold earrings. Her arm was hooked with her husband's. Gretchen's husband was a stout bald man who would yell things to the judges when they were taking notes on our gingerbread houses. Gretchen would give him angry glances every once in a while in response.

I didn't know the ins and outs of their marriage, but I got the feeling that Gretchen was the one who wore the pants in their relationship.

I nodded as we passed on the street, but she pretended not to see me, keeping her nose high in the air.

I swear, the woman would drown if a rainstorm hit.

Gretchen was a piece of work, all right.

But she didn't have to say hi to me. She'd hear me loud and clear, soon enough. She wouldn't be able to ignore me then.

I walked on, picking up the pace.

It was a dark winter's night, and I could feel the chills coming on. I pulled my down jacket tighter around me. All the storefronts were brightly lit with old-fashioned red and green bulbs, trying to instill the holiday spirit.

The longer I lived here, the more immune I became to that spirit.

It made me sad. I didn't want to be bitter about Christmas or holiday cheer. But maybe that's what happens when you live in a town where it's Christmas year-round. Christmas just doesn't mean the same.

Or at least it hadn't for the past two years.

I pushed on the heavy doors of the tavern and was greeted with a burst of warm, fermented air. I made my way to the bar at the back. The place I knew Warren would be.

"Hey there, Cin," Harold said, catching my eye from behind the bar. "What can I get you?"

"Aw, nothing for me tonight," I said. "I've got some more work to do back at the shop. I'm just here for the old man."

"The clock's struck 12, boys," Warren said from his crowded table, taking a long drink from his pint of beer.

I wondered how many that was for him. He was drinking more lately, and he really shouldn't have been. I was pretty sure his doctor would have been harassing me if she found out how much Warren was drinking. But I knew that coming down to the tavern, drinking with the boys and reminiscing about the old days at the lumber mill was one of the things that kept him going.

"How's the shop these days, Cinnamon?" Larry, my grandfather's best friend of nearly 55 years, asked.

"It's been a good season so far," I said. "How's Sheila? Is she ready for the Gingerbread Junction?"

"The house has smelled like gingerbread for days," Larry said, rubbing his wrinkled face and sighing.

"And that's a bad thing?" I asked.

"It's been torture. The woman won't let me even try any of it. I swear, I feel like she's watching me all the time, making sure I don't take any of her gingerbread." Larry said.

Warren started laughing, his whole body shaking. I shook my head.

"Well, Sheila means business," I said. "I look forward to seeing her at the competition."

"I'll just be glad when it's all over," Larry said. "Cruel, inhumane woman."

Warren finished the last of his beer.

"One of these days you're gonna have to learn to stand up to her, Larry," Warren said getting up off the barstool.

"It's too late for that," Larry said. "I'm about a century too old to change my ways."

"Isn't that the truth. Well, I'll see all you degenerates tomorrow," Warren said.

I waved goodbye. I hooked Warren's arm to help him. As we walked away, I noticed a man sitting at a table in the corner. He was maybe in his thirties and he had a thick, dark beard. A cowboy hat sat on the table next to the double shot of whiskey he was holding. He was staring at the shot glass like he had a lot on his mind.

I didn't recognize him, but he didn't look like an average tourist. The Pine Needle Tavern didn't get many tourists, anyway—it had "local" written all over its aging paneled walls and sticky floors.

The man sitting at the table lifted his eyes for a moment and our eyes locked.

Then, he quickly looked away, like the moment hadn't ever happened.

It left me with a strange feeling that followed me all the way out to the street.

CHAPTER 4

I drove Warren back home in my black Ford Escape. He liked walking to the tavern for his daily exercise, and then I would pick him up and drop him back at our house. When we got home, I made sure he took his pills and then set him up in front of the television to watch *Where Eagles Dare,* one of his favorite movies. He said I worked too much for a young beautiful woman. I rolled my eyes and then pecked him on the cheek. Then, I drove back to the shop.

I thought about Warren on the way over. I worried about him a lot lately. It wasn't just the drinking, either. He was getting old and that worried me.

My grandfather and I were close. He'd raised me since I was 13. After my mother died, a lot could have gone differently for me. I was on the brink of going down a bad path. Warren looked out for me and made sure I stayed right. In the meantime, he taught me how to play poker and how to build a fire without using matches, and how to survive if I ever got lost in the woods.

But he was forgetting things lately. Sometimes he'd be as sharp as a blackberry bush thorn. But every once in a while, he'd lose track of something.

Once, last year, he left one of the burners on after cooking breakfast. It nearly caused a fire at his house.

Since then, I'd been doing my best to take care of him. He'd moved in with me, even though he protested. He said he didn't want to burden me and that he didn't need someone to watch him all the time. But it wasn't a burden, and I liked having him close by. Just in case.

I still worried about him a lot, though.

I pulled up to the shop and got out of the car. I was met by a sharp and bitter wind.

The streets were dead as dead could be. I still had a lot of pies left to make for tomorrow morning. Starting on this year's gingerbread house had really cut into my time.

I sighed as I opened the front door of the shop. I didn't mind going back and putting in the extra hours. It was my own business after all, and I was grateful that it was doing so well. But I really needed to hire some help. I didn't know if I'd be able to survive the season by myself in the shop.

I went inside, locked up the front door, and hung my jacket and scarf up on the coat rack. I stamped my boots free of snow, and then went in the kitchen to get down to business.

I turned the lights on, put some Otis Redding, The Four Tops, and Harold Melvin & the Blue Notes on the speakers to get me energized, and wrapped an apron around my waist. I pulled out the pie dough that had been sitting in the fridge since I'd made it earlier that morning. I pre-heated the ovens, and rolled out the crusts, taking care not to touch the dough too much with my hands. That was a secret my mom passed down to me. If you touch the pie dough too much, the oils in your hands will affect the flakiness of the baked crust.

I rolled out crusts for seven pies. I draped them over the tin pans, pressing them lightly into the bottoms and then cutting the overhang around the rim.

I whistled to *Pain in My Heart*. I kept stealing glances at the unfinished gingerbread house in the corner, making mental notes about additions that I needed to make. Kara and I had decided on the theme of a Western Christmas for the gingerbread mansion. It wasn't that original of an idea, but it would be a winner with the judges. This was Central Oregon, after all. People loved their Western heritage here. Plus, we could add enough touches—enough peppermint candy boot spurs and licorice sheriff's badges and marzipan Appaloosa horses and gingerbread sheriffs—to make it really special and unique.

I put the pans in the oven to pre-cook the crusts, and then started making the fillings. I was planning on making two Mountain Blueberry Cinnamons, three Christmas River Cherries, a Lemon Gingercrisp, and if I had time, a Moundful Marionberry.

I started on the blueberry filling first, mixing together the blueberries, brown sugar, cinnamon and corn starch.

I caught my reflection in the glass pane of the window, suddenly.

I wasn't looking that bad. My long brown hair was pulled back in a loose-fitting pony tail, and my bangs had maintained their shape throughout the day of hard work. I looked a little pale, but I was wearing a black sweater that seemed to bring the pale out in me. Plus, it was winter. I always got as pale as a vampire during the winter in the Central Oregon mountains.

As I mixed the pie filling, I thought about Maui. I thought about those warm sands, and the feeling of the hot sun browning my skin. Of the sound of the wind in the palm trees.

I couldn't wait. I glanced at the gingerbread house base in the corner, and felt hopeful.

I suddenly heard a noise at the back door, and stopped mixing. I put down the spoon, and went to the door to look out into the blackness of the night.

I looked down to where the noise had come from.

It was the dog.

Huckleberry had come back.

His fur was dirtier than the last time I had seen him, and there was more desperation in his eyes. He was whining, too. A high-pitched whine that would have melted the coldest of hearts.

And it was starting to snow out there. Large flakes of crystalized snow sailed through the air, carried by a wicked winter wind.

I went to the front and got the pan of leftover strawberry rhubarb pie from the glass case, and went back. I opened the door slowly, trying not to scare him, but it didn't work. He bolted away into the black woods.

I wedged the pan into the snow on the back porch. The

snow was getting blown sideways, and I wished so very much that Huckleberry would stop his skittish protest and just come inside for the night.

It sent a chill through my heart to think of him out in the cold snow, wandering those dark woods.

I called out for him, my voice carried off by the cold north wind into the woods.

"Come here, Huckleberry!" I yelled. "Come here, pooch!"

There was no sign of him, though. I started stepping back inside the shop, when suddenly I saw a shadow moving through the trees in the distance.

I squinted into the swirling snow.

"Come here, Huckl—"

The words got caught in my throat and was replaced with a muffled cry.

The shadow in the woods wasn't Huckleberry.

Or any kind of animal for that matter.

It was a man.

I rushed back inside and locked the door, my mind racing with fear.

I'd suddenly stepped into a horror movie. The shadow in the woods was lumbering through the snow, and it looked like he was coming toward the shop.

"Damn it," I said out loud.

Christmas River was a safe place—most of the time. But it was just like any other Oregon town bordering the boonies. Everybody knew about the meth houses out in the depths of the Oregon woods. Everybody had seen those kind of people come to town every once in a while.

I was a tough girl, but seeing a strange man in the woods behind my shop was enough to jar me. Hell, it would have jarred most people.

I turned off the lights in the kitchen and rushed for my cell. I pressed 9-1-1 into the keypad and hesitated before pressing send. The man was just about up on the back porch now.

My heart was racing out of control as I heard his heavy footsteps coming up the back steps.

"Hello?" a faint voice, muffled by the wind, said. "Is anybody there?"

I shivered. I didn't know if I should answer. It was obvious that somebody was here, and he knew that. He would have seen the light go out.

"Hello?"

I took a deep breath and tried to steady my voice.

"Stay where you are," I yelled through the glass, showing myself, and making sure that he saw the phone in my hands.

He walked up to the glass to get a better look inside. And through the heavy snowfall, I got a better look at who he was.

I gazed at his face for a moment.

And when I recognized him, the phone slid out of my hand, hitting the cold tile floor with a crash.

CHAPTER 5

"What are you doing here?" I yelled through the glass.

"I... uh..." he started, pulling his cowboy hat off. "I followed the dog. Then I saw this place."

I could almost smell the whiskey through the pane. I could tell by his glazed eyes and confused expression that he was inebriated.

Big flakes of snow were falling into his hair and his thick beard. He shook with a visible chill, but he tried to hide it.

I let out a sigh of relief and wiped my sweaty hands on my apron.

I looked hard at him, sizing him up.

I had the advantage now. I knew who he was.

And because I had that advantage, I decided to do something I wouldn't normally have.

I decided to open the door.

I picked up the battered phone, put it in my jean pocket, and unlocked the door. I opened it slowly, cautiously.

He looked at me. He was surprised.

I got the sense he had no idea who I was.

"Do you want to come in?" I asked.

"What is this place?" he said.

I held the door open for him and he stepped inside, shaking the snowflakes from his hair.

He looked around slowly, like he couldn't believe what he was seeing.

"I followed the dog through the woods," he said, again. "And I saw this place… and it looked like heaven from out there. It smells like it too."

I smiled nervously.

"It's my pie shop," I said.

"It's beautiful," he said, slurring a little. "It's so warm in here."

"Why were you following the dog?" I asked.

"I was coming out of the tavern and I saw him," he said, still looking around in awe. "He looked like a stray. I wanted to catch him and bring him home."

"I've been trying to lure him in for the past two weeks," I said. "With no luck. But he keeps coming back here for scraps."

"I can see why," he said, looking around some more. "It smells like… like home in here."

He looked at me for a moment, his bleary eyes locking into mine. I was waiting for him to say something. To say my name. For a look of recognition to pass over his face, and for him to smile at me.

But the recognition never came. Just an awkward silence, and a gaze that lasted a little too long.

And then he seemed to come out of his drunkenness a little bit.

"I should go," he said. "You look busy and I'm taking up too much of your time."

"No," I said, the words slipping out of my mouth without my permission. "Stay until... until you can see straight, at least."

He laughed.

"I'm sorry. I must stink of it."

"Well, it doesn't take a rocket scientist to see you've had a few. Can I take your jacket?"

He looked at me, confused for a moment. Like he didn't know why I was being so nice to him, a strange man who'd nearly scared me half to death a few moments earlier.

He hadn't realized it yet, but he wasn't any stranger.

He took off his heavy, buffalo plaid jacket and handed it to me, hesitating a little. I took it from him along with the cowboy hat in his hands, and brought them out to hang in the front room coat rack. When I came back, I saw him looking intently at the gingerbread house in the corner.

"This is something else," he mumbled. "Did you make this?"

I nodded, going for the oven doors and checking on the pie crusts. They were just about ready.

"That's incredible," he said. "Ha! Is that the sheriff?" he said, pointing to a small, decorated gingerbread man coming down the steps of the unfinished mansion.

I grinned.

Usually, we waited until right before the competition to start making the embellishments and decorations like that. But earlier that afternoon, I had worked on a few sheriff prototypes. They turned out so well, I added them to the partially-built house.

"Sure is. The sheriff's heading into work. Can't be letting those hooligans paint the town red, now, can he?"

That made him laugh some. He shook his head.

"But what's this house doing here in the corner, all lonesome and sad-looking? It should be where people can see it."

"It's not done yet," I said. "It'll be a few days before it's complete."

"Ohhh," he said, like he understood. "You're one of those gingerbread competition ladies, aren't you?"

I laughed.

"Guilty as charged."

"I used to know a girl once who entered every year," he said. "But that was a long, long time ago."

I was quiet. He still didn't recognize me.

"Are you hungry?" I asked.

His eyes wandered over to the brightly lit oven.

"Starved," he said.

CHAPTER 6

Daniel Brightman sat at the kitchen island and ate the reheated slice of Christmas River Cherry pie in the same way that Huckleberry ate it.

Like he hadn't eaten in weeks.

Something about watching him eat the pie like that was oddly satisfying. I hadn't seen anybody eat one of my pies like that in a long, long time. The customers were usually self-conscious, eating the pie neatly, bite by bite, afraid that if they didn't someone might think they were a pig.

But Daniel was scarfing it down, like he was in love with every bite.

Maybe it was because he was drunk, but I liked that he didn't seem to care. He ate it the way he felt.

Starved.

I sat across from him, drinking a cup of pomegranate tea and waiting for the oven timer to go off so I could take the pies out and call it a night.

I watched him silently, hardly able to believe that he was sitting there in front of me.

He looked a little older, but not in a bad way. Just more mature. His beard had completely thrown me when I first saw him in the tavern earlier. But when I saw his eyes—those same light green eyes that he'd always had—I'd recognized him immediately. Well, almost immediately.

But he still had yet to remember me.

"I thought the dog was a wolf," Daniel said in between bites. "He was just there in the woods, staring at me."

"Really?" I said.

He shrugged.

"And I had nothing better to do, I guess. My gut told me he wanted me to follow him. And I ended up here."

"Yeah, he keeps showing up here at night lately."

"I don't blame him," Daniel said, smiling and finishing off the last giant forkful of pie. "When I saw the lights from the woods, I wondered if I hadn't froze out there, and if I hadn't just wandered into heaven."

I shook my head and tried to suppress a smile. It sounded like a line out of a bad novel, but he had said it with such sincerity, I just couldn't laugh at it.

"He's a hard dog to catch," I said. "He doesn't seem to trust me quite yet."

"He'll come around," Daniel said. "Especially if you keep feeding him so well."

He looked up, his eyes lingered on me, then he cleared his throat and looked back down.

"So how long have you been running this place?" he asked. "I don't remember ever seeing it when I used to live here."

"About five years," I said. "I moved back here with… well, about five years ago from Portland."

"Do you like what you do?" he asked.

I smiled, looking around the quaint, cozy kitchen that held all my dreams.

The place that had been my rock, my true source of strength, for the past two years.

"I don't get as much sleep as I used to," I said. "The hours are long. I'm here early in the morning and late at night. But at the end of the day, it's all worth it. You know what I mean? All the bad stuff just melts away because I belong doing this."

He looked up and smiled like he understood what I was talking about.

"Plus, you get to have drunk bums who show up on your doorstep in the middle of the night, scaring you half to death," he said. "You probably don't get that in your average 9 to 5 job."

I laughed.

"Yeah," I said. "I guess you could call it a perk. Homeless dogs and bums arriving at my doorstep in the middle of the night. Definitely didn't get that at my advertising firm job in Portland."

"Is that where you're from?" he asked. "Portland?"

I hesitated. Thinking about whether I should tell him who I was. But then, I decided not to. He'd figure it out in his own good time.

"No. I'm not from Portland," I said, clearing my throat. I went back over to the oven, checking the pies. The lattice on top was turning a nice golden brown, and the fruit filling was starting to bubble. They needed a couple more minutes and they'd be ready.

I turned back around. He was looking at me with that same expression of drunken awe.

"The smell is murder," he said, shaking his head. "How do you not just sit here and eat pie all day long?"

"Well, I won't lie. I used to be a few pounds lighter," I said, smiling.

"Well, you look great to me," he said.

The comment filled me with a sort of vain happiness. I quickly shooed it away, though. He was just being nice.

I walked back over to the kitchen island and took a seat on the barstool.

"So, stranger. What do you do?" I asked.

"Me?" he said. "I thought you'd have guessed it by now. I'm a professional pie-taster."

That made me laugh. He looked back at me with a straight face.

"No, really," he said. "You laugh, but I'm very distinguished. I'm constantly traveling from town to town, dispensing my wealth of knowledge to bakers around the world. I'm very well-known in some circles, you know."

"Lucky me," I said. "Of all the shops you could have stumbled into tonight, you found mine."

"I'm beginning to think this is fate," he said.

"You believe in such things?" I asked.

"Of course," he said. "Don't you?"

The timer went off. I went to the oven and put on my pair of mitts and took out the pies.

"No," I said. "Fate's just something invented to make us feel better about the crazy things that happen in our lives."

I placed the pies on a cooling rack and turned off the oven.

"It's hard to believe that a person who owns a pie shop and builds gingerbread houses and listens to Otis Redding doesn't believe in a little magic."

I shrugged.

"Well, I'm not your average gal, I guess."

"No," he said. "I'm beginning to see that."

I felt chills run down the back of my spine.

But they weren't the bad chills I usually got.

These were different.

He stood up from the kitchen island.

"Now I've really taken up too much of your time," he said. "I better leave."

"How are you getting home?" I asked. "You can't drive."

"I'll walk," he said. "It's not coming down as hard as it was."

I looked outside. Snow was coming down in droves out there, and the wind chimes in the back rang out in the fierce gusts.

"Get your coat," I said. "I'll give you a ride."

He tried to protest, but I wouldn't hear of it.

CHAPTER 7

He gave me directions, but I remembered where the Brightman house was.

I wanted to ask him what he was doing back here, but on the drive home, he'd fallen quiet. I figured the booze was wearing off, and he was getting sleepy. I pulled up to his house. The lights were all out.

He looked over at me for a brief moment before getting out of the car.

"I've taken advantage of your kindness," he said, looking guilty.

"No," I said. "I would've felt rotten if you'd passed out in the snow and frozen on the walk home. This isn't kindness. It's just me trying to make sure nobody dies."

"I don't want you to be sad," he said suddenly.

He said it in a serious tone that was unexpected.

I looked over at him, confused.

Was that the whiskey talking?

"What?" I said.

"I don't want you to be sad anymore," he said. "I see that you are. I don't know why you are, but I don't want you to be. You're too…"

He trailed off and looked over at me with his deep-set eyes, holding my stare for a moment. Then he suddenly opened the car door and got out.

"Goodnight," he said. "And thank you, miss."

He tipped his hat as he said it.

"Okay," I said. "Goodnight Daniel."

He shut the door and then stood in the snow, looking at me through the car window for a moment.

He was realizing that he'd never told me his name, I could tell.

I drove away down the icy, deserted street, leaving him behind to think it out in the snowstorm.

The entire way home, his words haunted me, leaving me with an unsettled feeling.

I don't want you to be sad anymore…

I didn't like that he could read me so easily.

CHAPTER 8

I went to sleep that night, thinking of days that felt so distant in my memory, it was like they belonged to another lifetime.

Thinking back to those long summers when I was a teenager. Driving down forest back roads with the radio turned way up, rooting for the Christmas River High boys of summer while they circled the bases, and spending the evenings out under a blanket of stars.

I had never been a carefree person. The death of my mother at an early age took care of that. But those summers were the closest thing I've ever felt to being carefree. Those long, lazy summers where the woods would burst to life under the hot sun. Where the nights would be short and magical and filled with bright moonlight.

It was during one of those summer nights when I first met Daniel Brightman. I mean, when I first really met him.

He was two grades above me at Christmas River High. I'd known of him and seen him in the halls before. He was tall, even back then, with dark hair and bright green eyes, and a crooked nose, the result of breaking it one too many times while playing baseball. In the halls, I never saw him without a guitar slung over his back.

I was an awkward teenager. I hardly socialized, and Kara was really my only friend. I was shy. Painfully shy. I was still dealing with the death of my mother and the feelings of being lost and unsure in the world. I didn't get along with many other kids.

But one evening, Kara dragged me down to The Burned Tree, a place by the lake where high school kids liked to hang out and drink and make-out around a big fire underneath a large pine that had been hit by lightning. It wasn't my scene, to the say the least. In fact, it scared me. But Kara wanted to go meet up with Billy Sanders, a boy she'd been chasing for half the summer, and she needed me as her wing man. Or wing girl.

When we pulled up that late August night, I immediately wished we hadn't. I didn't belong there. I didn't belong with the Callie Bennetts or the Julia Mathesons—the girls who had fathers who were real estate developers or lawyers. Who got cars for their 16th birthdays, and walked around school like they owned it. The kind of girls who only spent time outdoors if boys were going to be there.

The kind of girls who had mothers to teach them about how to put on make-up and curl their hair.

Kara was pretty, and could pass with them. But not me. No. I didn't belong with them, or with the boys that were there either. I stuck out like a sore thumb. Like a homeless person at a charity ball. Like a beat-up Hyundai in a parking lot full of Porsches. Like a pair of weathered Reebok sneakers next to shiny Air Jordans in a shoe closet.

I sat alone most the night, staring at the campfire, wondering why I'd let Kara drag me there.

But then, a pickup truck pulled up, and a boy got out and pulled his guitar from the flatbed, and he walked over and sat down, and mesmerized everyone there with his playing and singing.

And when he stopped playing, the Julia Mathesons and Callie Bennetts all wanted to talk with him. But from across the flickering flames of the campfire, I noticed that he kept looking over at me.

Not at them. At *me.*

At first I didn't believe it. But as the night wore on and people started leaving or finding more secluded places to make-out, Daniel Brightman got up, walked around the fire, and took a seat right next to me.

And he talked to me. Really talked to me. He asked me questions about my life and what I liked doing and what I wanted to do someday. I told him about playing poker with my grandfather and hiking in the woods and making gingerbread houses for the competition each year. He told me about his dad, that he didn't get along with him, and how his mom had left them a long time ago. He knew a little bit about what I was going through. He knew what it was like not to have a mom around.

He started strumming on his guitar, playing an old song from the 70s. I'd heard the song before, but never heard it sung so sweetly.

It was like it wasn't even the same song.

And I soon realized that we were the only ones left sitting

around the dying campfire. Everyone, including Kara, had left.

But I wasn't angry at her. I might have been at another time during the night, but I wasn't then.

I remember the fire died out, white smoke curling up into the blackness. Daniel put his guitar down, and took my hand, and we walked down to the lake, the waves gently lapping up on the sandy shore.

A crack of thunder lit up the night sky suddenly, and I jumped.

He grabbed a hold of me and pulled me close. Suddenly, I was looking up into his pale green eyes, and he was smiling at me.

"Don't be afraid," he said.

I started saying something stupid. That the thunder didn't scare me. That I spent half of my waking hours out in these woods. That I wasn't a typical girl who needed a boy to tell me not to be afraid of the thunder.

But I didn't get a chance to say any of that. Because Daniel Brightman brought me closer to him and kissed me.

One of those kisses that no matter how long you live, you never forget. Because for once in your life, you're in the moment. Completely and totally and absolutely living in that very moment, with no thoughts about anything or anyone else except him.

And that's how Daniel Brightman stole my heart, all those years ago.

We talked a little more that night, and then it started to rain. We ran to his truck, and he gave me a ride home.

He promised he would call me the next day, and that we'd go to Christmas River High's pre-season football game together the next weekend.

When he dropped me off, I thought my heart might just about burst out of my chest with joy.

I was young and impressionable then. I realize that now. It was young love, if even that yet. It had just barely started to bloom.

But it's strange how things are. In that moment, I felt more than I'd ever felt since. Even when I met Evan, it wasn't the same feeling. The same feeling of delirious happiness and wild abandon.

Probably only 16 year olds had feelings like that. First loves only had feelings like that.

But I'd never get a chance to find out what could have been.

After he didn't call the next day, I asked around. I heard a few days later that his brother, who was four years older than him and living in California, had died after being shot in a convenience store by a robber.

They didn't have the funeral in Christmas River. His dad didn't want it that way for some reason.

Last I heard of Daniel Brightman, he had gone to California to bury his brother.

And then, I never heard anything about him again.

He disappeared. Almost as though he had never existed. Into thin air. Dropping out of high school, dropping out of all of our lives.

I tried calling him, but he never answered.

After a few months, I gave up on him. My first impression of love and first impression of heartbreak happened one after the other.

Evan and I got together after a Christmas River High basketball game that winter, and I rarely thought about Daniel after that.

I figured he walked out of my life forever then.

But I was wrong.

I stared at the ceiling and yawned, thinking about what a strange world it was.

Of all the stores and shops downtown that he could have ended up at tonight, he ended up at mine.

Maybe in the morning, when the booze wore off, he'd finally remember me.

CHAPTER 9

Even after several years of owning a pie shop, leaving a warm bed at five in the morning was a bitch.

Especially after working long hours the day before.

I dragged myself out of bed, wrapping my plaid robe tightly around my body, trying to stamp out the chill.

I pulled back the curtains in my room, and looked outside at the dark street. It was something that was left over from childhood, when you'd check to see if it snowed enough for the schools to cancel class.

But these days, I checked to see if the conditions were drivable, not to see if I was lucky enough to get a snow day.

It had really come down the night before. In the light of the streetlamps, I could make out a thick layer of snow, covering the streets and sidewalks and trees like a thick layer of buttercream frosting.

I'd have to do some heavy duty shoveling before I could even get out to the street.

Luckily, the driveway was short, and shoveling was a good way to get in some early morning exercise. Exercise was something I never had time for anymore. I needed it to be worked into my day in a practical way.

Suddenly, the words Daniel Brightman had said the night before echoed in my ears, coming from out of nowhere.

You look good to me he had said, after I told him that I'd gained some weight since opening the shop.

It made me smile in the early morning darkness. But I quickly quashed the absurd, giddy feeling that arose from the memory.

For all I knew about Daniel Brightman these days, he could have been married.

Plus, I should have still been mad at him. Mad that he never returned any of my phone calls. That he'd left me behind in the dust all those years ago. Plus he didn't even remember me. Like what had happened between us didn't matter to him. Like he didn't remember that kiss at all.

As I walked out of my room and downstairs, I thought about how things could have turned out had Daniel stayed in Christmas River. Maybe Evan and I wouldn't have ever started dating. Maybe instead of marrying Evan, it would have been Daniel that I married.

Maybe my life would have turned out a lot different.

But I couldn't think in those terms. In the what-ifs, and could've beens, and if-only's. Life was tumultuous and unpredictable and volatile. There was no use in dwelling on the way things could have turned out. It only made for regrets.

I got downstairs, and Warren was at the kitchen stove, dressed in his trademark green flannel shirt.

From the incredible aromas rising up from the frying pan, I knew what he was doing.

"You know what Doctor Koehler would say about that," I said as I pulled down two mugs from the cupboard.

"Don't I know it," Warren said, adding some pepper to the crackling bacon in the pan. "That German she-devil wench is trying to kill me with all that Melba toast crap."

I couldn't help grinning. That was a good way of describing her, but that didn't make her wrong.

"You've heard what she said about my drinking, right? Two or three drinks a week at the most. Can you believe that? Who does she think I am, a Shih Tzu lap dog?"

"She's only looking out for you," I said, pouring him a steaming cup of coffee and placing it on the counter next to him. "So am I, old man. I don't want you keeling over. Not anytime soon."

"I will if I'm forced to eat that health food crap and cut down on my drinking," he said. "Quality over quantity of life. Am I right, Cinny?"

I sighed, taking a sip of my coffee. It was bitter and strong, and was just what was needed at 5:15 on a dark winter morning.

"Just try to substitute a few meals with some of that stuff, would ya?" I said. "I'll come back at lunch time and make you a salad. What about that? It'll be good, I promise."

"You've got enough to do today without being my personal chef," he said. "Besides, I'm going to lunch with Bob Gerity this afternoon. He's back in town for a few days."

"Well can you order a salad or something?" I said. "For me, at least?"

"I don't want Bob thinking I've gone soft in my old age," he said, collecting the bacon from the pan and placing it on some paper-towels for it to drain. "I'll try again at dinner."

"You promise?" I said.

He nodded.

"Okay, then," I said, finishing the last of the coffee, catching a few bitter grinds from the bottom. "I've got to go shovel. It snowed like crazy last night."

I placed the mug in the sink and left Warren to eat his highly prized bacon in peace. I glanced at the stove, to make sure he'd turned it off. He had. I went upstairs, changed, and came back downstairs ready to combat the field of snow that my driveway had turned into overnight. It took me about half an hour of heavy lifting, but I finally cleared out the drifts to create a path out to the street. By the time I was finished, I was a sweaty mess.

I went back upstairs and took a shower. Then I got ready, staring at myself a little bit longer than usual in the mirror. Wondering if I really did look that different from the girl that Daniel knew all those years ago.

And to see whether or not he was right. If I did indeed look sad, or if I had just been tired from overwork last night when he had said that.

But in the end, I couldn't really tell.

I finally pulled on my pea coat and hat and gloves, and went downstairs. Warren was watching an early morning show on the weather channel that showed people in New York dressed in shorts and t-shirts after a spell of unusually warm December weather there.

New York could have been on another planet, the way it was here.

"Be careful out there, Cinny," Warren said as I kissed the top of his balding head goodbye. "Oh, and I was wondering if you could pick me up from the tavern again tonight? The boys are throwing a welcome-home party for Bob."

I sighed. So much for the healthy dinner. It would be wiped out entirely by a few rounds of carb-heavy beer.

Warren looked up, noticing my hesitation.

"Oh, c'mon, Cinny. Don't worry so much. I'm gonna outlive you. Just you wait and see."

I shook my head.

"What time, old man?" I asked.

"The usual," he said.

I nodded silently and left.

One of these days, I was going to have to lay down the law. I knew that. Before something bad happened.

But the old man loved his food and he loved his beer. Quality over quantity, he'd said.

I drove over to work, slowly through the empty streets thick with snow, thinking about Warren, and how we were all getting old.

CHAPTER 10

Kara came into the shop later that morning in a huff, after I'd put a few more pies in the oven and served dozens of tourists coffee and pie.

"I'm glad you're here. You'll never believe who I saw last night," I said. "How'd it go, by the way?"

Today was the entrance day for the gingerbread competition. Usually, Kara and I would go over to the Culinary School building together and enter, but these days, I didn't have any bakery assistants to take over for the morning hours at the shop. Hadn't had any for nearly two years.

So Kara kindly volunteered to enter for us.

But she came into the pie shop, stomping her heels loudly against my tile floor, feeling like a gust of crazy south wind. There was a wild energy about her, and her blue eyes were large and enraged-looking.

"Can I talk to you in the back?" she said in a low, serious voice.

"What's wrong?" I said.

The thought crossed my mind that something went wrong at the registration. That maybe there were too many people registering and we were bumped out.

I nodded, and took off my apron. I turned the front sign around, saying that I'd just stepped away and would be right back. I looked around the dining room, making sure everybody was content and didn't need any more coffee.

Then I followed Kara back to the kitchen.

"I'm so angry, Cin, I could just rip that witch's head off!" Kara yelled, a little bit too loudly.

I was pretty sure all the customers heard her profane outburst.

"What are you talking about?" I said. "What's going on?"

She took a deep breath, trying to collect herself. Her face was starting to turn a bright red.

"I debated about whether I should tell you," she said, pacing back and forth, her heels clicking against the floor. "But I knew you'd find out sooner or later. I figured it's better to tell you now than for you to find out the day of competition, right? Better know what to expect than—"

"Tell me what, Kara?" I said, giving her a sharp look that made her stop in mid-pace.

She looked down and sighed, taking a moment to collect herself. My heart was about to beat out of my chest while I waited.

"She's entering this year," she said in a low, shaky voice. "The witch is *competing*."

The oven timer went off, blending with the ear-splitting sound of alarms going off in my head.

Kara hadn't mentioned her by name, but I knew who she was talking about.

The room started to spin suddenly. I grabbed a hold of the kitchen island and steadied myself. Kara rushed up to me, ready to catch me if I fainted like a southern belle.

But I wasn't going to faint. I was stronger than that. But I couldn't deny that the news shook me up.

Shook me up real bad.

"Sit down, honey," Kara said, grabbing a kitchen stool and pulling it up for me. She had gone from infuriated to gentle in the span of a few seconds.

"Are you sure?" I finally croaked out as I stared out the window, watching the peaceful trees sway in the wind. The exact opposite of how I felt inside.

She nodded.

"I'd recognize that bleached, curly air-head blond hair anywhere," she said. "And that smug smile. Damn it, Cin, she was so smug."

I gripped the cold table as hard as I could.

"And when she saw that it was just me there, it was almost like she was disappointed or something," Kara said. "Like she wanted you to be there and see that she was entering in the competition."

"But why?" I said. "Why is she doing this?"

Kara shook her head.

"Because she's a greedy harpy," Kara said. "You'd think it'd be enough that she stole…"

Kara trailed off, peering at my face. I was trying so hard to keep it together. So very, very hard to be the strong person that I'd always prided myself in being. In being the strong person that I wanted to be. Logical and clearheaded and collected.

But when it came to *her*, I just couldn't do it. I couldn't keep it together.

I started trembling feverishly with those chills. Those bad chills that came whenever I remembered it all.

"Why…" I started again. "Why would…"

My voice broke, and the tears started streaming down my cheeks.

"You poor girl," Kara said, walking around the table and hugging me. "I'm so sorry. I shouldn't have told you. I just thought—"

"No," I said, in between sobs. "You were right to tell me. I would have wanted to know."

We were quiet while I let out a few more embarrassing sobs.

"Don't worry, hon," Kara said. "We're going to murder that competition. We're going to paint the walls of our gingerbread house with her blood."

That made me laugh in a kind of devastated, out-of-control way. Kara was always good with her dramatics and never failed to make me feel better when I was down.

In this case, way down.

"That witch is going to be sorry," Kara said, handing me a Kleenex. "We'll make her sorry for everything's she's done to you."

I wiped my nose, and tried to collect myself.

For everything she's done to you…

The words echoed in my head.

There was a lot. A lot we had to make her sorry for.

"Don't you worry," Kara said again.

I stared out the window like a mental patient while Kara tried to tell me all the ways she would be sorry. After a few minutes, a burning smell hit my nostrils.

I shot up in a panic, running over to the oven. I opened it, pulling on a pair of oven mitts.

A wave of burnt smoke escaped the oven, hitting me in the face.

"Damn it!" I shouted, wanting to say something else. Something a little more descriptive.

I pulled out the burnt pies, their lattice tops a roasted shade of black.

They were beyond saving.

I looked back at Kara.

Even she couldn't pep-talk me out of this one.

She sighed.

"I'm so sorry, Cin," she said.

I placed the pies on the counter and rested my head in my hands.

"Who did you see last night?" she said, after a moment of devastated silence.

"What?" I said.

"When I first came in, you said that I'd never believe who you saw last night. Who'd you see?"

I sighed deeply.

"It doesn't matter," I said.

I stared at the burnt pies for a while, and then put three of them outside on the back patio.

At least Huckleberry would be happy tonight.

That would make one of us.

CHAPTER 11

When noon rolled around, I did something I rarely ever did. I put a sign out in front saying I'd be right back, and I closed up the shop for half an hour.

I readjusted my purple knit hat as I walked down Main Street and took a left on Holly Street. It had stopped snowing for the time being, and dark, dramatic clouds sailed briskly across the sky, revealing pockets of blue as they spread and pulled apart. Sometimes the sun would come out for a few moments before hiding behind the clouds again.

Half way to the bridge, I realized that I'd forgotten to wear my jacket and was only in my gray turtleneck. But I didn't feel cold. The air felt good and fresh and somehow cleansing in my lungs. It took away that burnt pie smell that the shop was now filled with.

I made it to the bridge and walked halfway across, stopping right in the middle.

I watched the river slowly meander beneath my feet. Sometimes in the summer, the Christmas River rushed by with a frenzied speed, like the water had places to go and wanted to get there as soon as it could. But as we got deeper into winter, it began to slow down, almost like a bear in hibernation. Soon, it would just be a trickle, the river falling asleep in winter's death grasp.

I watched the water, hypnotized by it for a while, trying to regain control of my thoughts. Trying to calm down and clear my head.

But it was hard.

It had come completely out of left field. I hadn't seen it coming.

I figured that she'd taken everything from me already. What more could she possibly do?

But I guess I had been wrong and Kara had been right.

She wasn't going to stop with stealing my husband.

Bailey, the woman who up until two years ago had been my bakery assistant and good friend, wanted to take the Gingerbread Junction Competition title away from me too.

I shuddered as a sharp and clean breeze cut through my sweater, touching my skin before moving on.

Bailey.

Sometimes I'd wake up in the middle of the night, questioning whether or not it all really happened.

Then I'd look at the other side of the bed, the side that had been cold and empty for two years, and I didn't have to question anymore.

The nightmare was real.

Evan, my high school sweetheart, my boyfriend all through college and my husband since the year after I graduated, the man I thought I was going to spend the rest of my life with, the man I thought I was going to grow old with, the man I thought I was going to retire in Hawaii with one day, had left me for another woman.

More than that, he'd left me for my bakery assistant and our friend, Bailey.

I hadn't seen that coming either. Not in a million years would I have guessed that.

I always liked to think I was a tough, no-nonsense, practical girl who had good instinct when it came to people. I used to think that women who didn't know that their husbands were cheating on them were either not paying attention, or were willingly blind to their betrayal.

But I was stupid. And oh-so-wrong.

There were signs, sure. But I trusted him. I'd always trusted him, since I was 16, I had. I didn't believe that was something he'd ever do. So when he'd stay out a little later with his buddies, or when he'd go on business trips for his job with the High Springs Lodge that lasted longer than he'd told me they would, or when he'd offer to give Bailey rides to work after her car broke down… I didn't see those signs. Any of them.

Because when you love and trust someone, you don't see signs as signs. You interpret them differently. He's just being a guy hanging out with his friends, or he's just a hard worker, or he's just looking out for a friend of ours.

I found out the first week of December two years ago that he'd been having an affair with Bailey.

It wasn't anything dramatic. I didn't walk in on them or anything.

It was almost as low key as a reveal of your husband

cheating on you could get.

It was the morning. He was in the shower and his phone buzzed, the way it did when he got a text message.

I don't know why I looked. It was just one of those things. It rang, and I checked it.

There wasn't even anything explicit or incriminating in the text message. But I knew it was from her.

Something just clicked. I couldn't explain it. But I just knew. At some higher level, I just knew.

When he got out of the shower, I confronted him. I had his phone and wouldn't give it back to him until he admitted what he had done.

He broke a lamp in our room and stormed out.

I spent the first weekend in December crying and screaming and yelling at him. And I made him tell me everything. Every last heart-wrenching detail.

It'd been going on for six months. He was going to tell me, he said. He was working his courage up to tell me.

But he was clearly a coward. Six months of working on his courage, and he never told me what he needed to.

Things just weren't the way they used to be, he said. He told me I'd been spending too much time at the shop and not spending enough time with him. He said I wasn't married to him anymore, not really. I was married to my business. He said I'd been pushing him away for years.

He said all these things, but none of them were the real reason he was leaving me. None of it was the real reason he'd started up an affair with a woman who had been one of our best friends.

I still didn't know what the real reason was. Maybe he just fell out of love with me. I didn't like to think that, but it might have been the truth.

When I finished yelling at him and throwing every curse word in the English language at him, I kicked him out of the house and told him I never wanted to see him. Ever.

And for the past two years, my wish had yet to come true, but it was beginning to. He still lived in the Christmas River area. With *her*. But after the divorce, I didn't run into him much, if at all. They'd moved closer to Metolius Valley, a town a little bigger than Christmas River about 20 minutes away. And for the time being, that seemed to be far enough.

I'd been doing my best to overcome it, to be the strong person I knew I was deep down, or at least the one I wanted to be. It hadn't been easy. The wound still felt fresh sometimes.

But I was doing better. My shop was doing great. I was getting along on my own just fine. I had the support of Warren and Kara, two people who had been my rocks through the divorce.

Sometimes I regretted things. Like making the decision to move from Portland back to Christmas River. Sometimes I thought we should have stayed in the city longer, maybe the boredom of a small town made him do things he might not have done otherwise. Maybe he felt suffocated here. Maybe he was right. I did love my business more than him. Maybe there was some truth to that.

Then I'd regain my senses, and realize that even if all that was true, there was still something else.

He'd still cheated on me. With my friend.

And there was no excuse in the world that would cover that one.

In the meantime though, I had made the life around me okay. I had made it bearable. I was getting better every day. I was starting to feel alive again. Starting to feel like I wasn't an inverted zombie, all dead and rotted on the inside. I had started to feel like maybe there was still hope for me.

Then… this had to happen. That homewrecker shows up at the one thing I take pride in, and tries to ruin it for me.

I wanted to wring her by her scrawny neck and scream at her at the top of my lungs *Haven't you done enough???*

An old couple walked behind me on the bridge, their heavy steps making the bridge shake. I leaned farther over the railing, not wanting to make eye contact. Being that it was a small town, the chances of me knowing them was pretty high, and I didn't feel in the mood to chat.

They passed by quickly, thankfully, and without any conversation.

I gripped the cold wooden railing, and bit down on my lip, an anger surging up from my core like a dragon.

She may have taken my husband. There was no contest there. I'd lost that battle, hands down.

But there was no way in the roaring fiery furnaces of hell that she was going to steal this gingerbread competition from me.

I took a deep breath and started walking. The cold was setting in, and I needed to get back to the shop.

I had a lot of work to do there.

CHAPTER 12

When I got back, John was waiting for me outside. His cheeks were bright red, like he'd been standing out in front of the closed sign since I left. In my shock, I'd forgotten that he showed up at the shop at exactly noon each day. You could set a timer to him.

"I'm so sorry, John!" I said, quickly pulling my keys out from my jean pocket and unlocking the front door. "I just needed some fresh air."

He nodded, rubbing his hands together for warmth. I held the door open for him and he walked in, taking his seat at the usual leather booth near the window. He took his beanie hat off, revealing his clean-cut graying hair.

I took my scarf off, and put it in the back. I quickly wrapped my frilly cowgirl apron around my waist, and came back out.

"The usual today?" I asked.

He nodded. He shook with a visible chill.

Needless to say, I felt rotten.

I went back behind the counter and pulled out the strawberry rhubarb pie, slicing it and placing it on one of the special holiday plates.

I only ever made the rhubarb pie for him these days. I myself had never been a big fan of that flavor combination, and it was rarely ever ordered by anybody else this time of year. But John was insistent on ordering it every time. I didn't know why. He never even finished it, and I got the impression he didn't even really like it. Or any other pie, for that matter.

Still, he was close to being my most loyal customer. I always made a point of having that pie in the shop.

"How's your day been so far?" I asked when I came around the counter with the plate and a mug of steaming coffee.

"It's been just fine," he said, clearing his throat. "A little chilly, but nothing I couldn't handle."

I clicked my tongue against the top of my mouth.

"Sorry about that again," I said, shaking my head. "I just felt like I needed to get out of the kitchen for a while."

He took a sip of his coffee. I went to the front and turned the sign around to say "open."

"Is something bothering you?" he asked.

I hesitated for a moment. I thought about telling him, but then something stopped me from doing it.

"I just burned a batch of pies by accident," I said. "It's just a real pain in the ass. I'm going to be here all night trying to make up for it."

"That doesn't sound like you," he said, playing with the piece of pie in front of him but not really eating it. "What happened?"

I sighed.

"I got distracted," I said.

I started to leave the table to take my place behind the counter when he stuck a hand out in front of my path to stop me.

He took another sip of his coffee and then cleared his throat free of phlegm.

"Listen," he said "I could help you, you know. I'm no Julia Child in the kitchen, but I'm not completely incompetent either. After I close up the practice tonight I could come back here and help you bake your pies."

Now it was my turn to clear my throat.

"Jeez," I said. "That's so kind of you, John, but I don't want to put you out like that. I'm the one that burnt the pies. It's my mess to clean up."

"You wouldn't be putting me out," he said. "It'd be my pleasure. Maybe I could take you to dinner afterwards."

My stomach started churning with uneasiness.

For nearly a year, I knew this day was coming. I also knew that when it did come, I'd be unsure what to do when he asked.

Like I said. I wasn't completely against the idea of Dr. John Billings. In fact, in a town this small, a lot of women would have thought I hit a homerun by nabbing a handsome doctor.

But I wasn't completely about the idea either. I didn't like him in that way. At least not yet, anyway.

"Well, that's just so nice," I said. "But I just… well, I wouldn't want to—"

The front doorbell jangled as a customer walked in.

I had never been so glad for an interruption in all my life.

"Just give me a minute," I said to John, placing a hand on his shoulder, a movement I immediately regretted because of what he probably interpreted it as.

I went around the back of the counter up to the cash register to meet the customer. I woke the register up by hitting one of the keys.

"What can I get you?" I said, looking up at the customer.

My heart jumped in my chest.

"Cinnamon Peters," he said, a broad smile on his face. "How the hell are you?"

CHAPTER 13

I was speechless for a moment.

And then, the nerves started up.

He took his hat off and smiled at me.

It was odd. The entire night before when Daniel Brightman had been in my kitchen, I hadn't been nervous in the least.

But now that he remembered who I was, my palms started getting sweaty and my heartbeat started picking up.

"You must think I'm a real fool," he said.

"Well, I…" I started saying. "I wouldn't call you that, but yeah… I won't lie. I was surprised you didn't recognize me."

"You wouldn't believe how tortured I was by it," he said. "When you left and I realized I hadn't told you my name, I just couldn't figure out how you knew me. I lay awake half the night trying to figure it out."

I looked past his shoulder for a second, noticing John turning to look at us. Eavesdropping on our conversation.

I cleared my throat.

"Well, what tipped you off, Sherlock?" I said.

He grinned. I noticed that he looked pretty good for

someone who should have had a hangover. If it had been me, I would have looked like a hot mess with dark rings around my eyes. But Daniel looked relaxed, easy, content. No sign of a hangover whatsoever.

"Well, I went through all the years that I lived here, going through the people I knew in each grade level of school," he said. "It took me until about three in the morning to get to the summer after junior year, but I got there in my own good time."

"That memorable, huh?" I said, raising my eyebrows and placing a hand on my hip.

"No, it's not that at all," he said. "Just… my memory works differently. And most the time I try not to think about the past. For a while, I tried to forget a lot of my growing up years. Some not so good memories there. But then when you block it all out, you lose some of the good, too."

I nodded. I guess that made sense. Maybe.

On my end, it hadn't taken nearly as long to remember him.

I thought back to his earlier question.

Was he a fool?

The verdict was still out on that one.

"But I remember you, Cinnamon," he said. "I don't want you to think I forgot about that night by the lake."

I could see John moving his head around at his table, trying to get a better eavesdropping angle.

I shifted my feet uncomfortably.

I really wished that Daniel would've come in at a different time.

"You know I called you," I said, clearing my throat. "You know that, right?"

He nodded solemnly.

"I wasn't in a good place then," he said. "I'm sorry if I hurt you."

"You didn't," I said, lying. "I was okay."

"Yeah," he said. "You seem to have done pretty good for yourself here."

I smiled.

"So, professional pie-taster, what in the hell are you doing back here? I thought I'd never see you again, the way you tore out of town."

"Well, my dad died three years ago," Daniel said.

"I'm sorry to hear that," I said.

Daniel's father had left Christmas River shortly after Daniel had, moving back east where his people were from. They still kept the house here, though, and occasionally, his dad would come back in town during the summer to go fishing. Three years ago, Walter Brightman's obituary ran in the Christmas River Weekly. I heard there was a memorial for him here for some of his friends, but that he was buried back east.

"Well, I haven't gotten a chance to take care of things here… you know, the house and everything. So I figured now was as good a time as any."

"How long are you here for?"

"I don't know," he said. "As long as it takes, I guess."

I was just about to ask Daniel where he'd been living and what he did now, when I saw John stand up and pull his beanie on.

He came over to us, walking up with a strange, aggressive gait.

"You let me know about tonight, Cinnamon," he said in an irritated tone, talking over Daniel. "Come over to the practice around 5 o'clock. Maybe we could do dinner first."

I nodded, and he walked away quickly and, I sensed, a little angrily.

We watched him open the door, walk out, and let the wind slam the door behind him. A cold gust ran through the dining room.

Daniel looked back at me.

"I hope I wasn't interrupting anything," he said.

I shook my head.

"No," I said. "It was nothing. So you don't know how long you're staying?"

"Through the holidays at least," he said. "But we'll see then. See where the road takes me."

"Do you have a job to go back to?" I asked.

The door jingled, and an army of old ladies with shopping bags suddenly entered the shop.

I sighed. I really wanted to talk more with him. I wanted to find out what he did, where he'd been all these years, and what he planned to do now that he was back here.

But I knew that the army of old ladies were going to squash any hope of catching up with Daniel Brightman.

He must have seen my exasperated expression.

He smiled at me. A warm smile that sent chills up my spine.

"Perils of the pie business," he said, nodding to the ladies behind him.

"Listen," he said, leaning across the counter. "I'd really

like to repay you for your kindness last night. I probably would be face down in the snow right about now if you hadn't rescued me. What about a drink tonight?"

My heart beat hard in my chest.

"That is, if you've forgiven me."

"Ma'am, does this blueberry pie have nutmeg in it too? Or just cinnamon?" one of the old ladies said in a raised voice, pointing at the glass case.

I looked back at Daniel, who was running a hand through his dark hair, waiting for me to answer.

"No. It'll be a long while before I forgive you, Daniel Brightman." I said.

His face fell a little bit and part of me enjoyed the moment. It was a little taste of his own medicine, but I didn't let it last too long.

"But… I'll let you make it up to me."

It only took me 1.2 seconds to decide that I was going to say yes to his offer.

No hesitation at all. No doubt. Nothing.

He tapped his cowboy hat on the counter and grinned.

"You're a kind woman," he said. "I'll pick you up at five?"

"Make it five thirty," I said.

"Ma'am?" the old woman said. "Can you give me an answer?"

Daniel winked at me, put on his hat, and walked out the front door.

And left me with the old women to tend to.

But I didn't mind them. I didn't even mind them calling me "Ma'am."

CHAPTER 14

John had left the majority of his strawberry rhubarb pie on the plate.

I felt a little guilty about the way Daniel had waltzed in here and stolen the show. I recognized that John had probably spent all year building up his courage, trying to work out a way to ask me out. He had finally found a moment when we were alone, and an innocuous way to spend time with me and ask me, and it had all been dashed.

I felt bad, but at the same time, I hadn't liked that tone he'd taken with me. Telling me to be there at his practice at five when I hadn't even said yes to his offer of help.

He'd said it in a petit tone, and it bothered me.

Yes, he'd been a regular customer, coming into my shop for a year now. But that didn't mean he owned me. I wasn't his property, which is the sense I got in his tone when he stomped out of here.

I told myself this, but it didn't help much with the guilt. Because no matter how I spun things, there was one thing that was true.

When John had asked me out, I hesitated. I hesitated because of the feeling in my gut that told me that I didn't like him that way, and that I most likely never would. No matter his kindness, or profession, or good looks, Dr. John Billings didn't elicit any feelings from me. No matter how much he wanted it.

On the other hand, When Daniel had asked me out for a drink, I didn't even have to think about it. I hadn't seen him in 17 years, but the answer was the same.

Yes.

That said something right there. That said that even if Daniel hadn't come into the shop this afternoon, I still shouldn't have accepted John's invitation to dinner.

There was no future there. That was clear now.

I would have to tell him that evening before Daniel stopped by. John might be angry, he might never come into my shop again, he might hate me.

But I needed to be honest with him. I owed him that much.

All was fair in love and war. That's what Kara had said, and she was right. I knew that, better than anyone. I'd been on the other end before.

And I owed myself what little happiness I could get. I'd been through hell in the past two years.

I talked myself into this as I waited for another batch of pies that I had made that afternoon to finish baking. They were meant to replace the burnt ones. It was late afternoon, and the long line of customers had all been helped, and the shop was mostly empty.

I had called Kara and told her that we'd have to work on the gingerbread mansion tomorrow rather than tonight. She said she understood and asked if I needed a girls' night. I thanked her, but told her that I had other plans. By the tone of her voice, I knew she wanted to ask more about those plans, but she dropped it, seeming to sense that I didn't want to talk about it. At least not yet.

Now, all I had to do was finish up baking the pies and cleaning up the shop, and then I'd go over to John's office and tell him.

My stomach turned just thinking about it. But that was what an honest, respectful person would do. He might hurt some, but it would save him some heartache in the long run.

I stopped for a moment, looking out the back window of the kitchen to admire the sunset.

It had stopped snowing briefly, and it was one of those early winter sunsets that turned the sky a flaming shade of pink and gold, and made the snow glow.

Whenever I started wondering about whether or not I should be living in a bigger city, and from time to time I did, I'd have a moment like this and realize that I was exactly where I should be.

Christmas River was a beautiful place to live. Nestled in the heart of the pristine Cascade Mountains, the woods and lakes around here were some of the loveliest in the country. And to me, in the world.

I knew a lot of people who grew up in small towns only wanted to run away from them, but not me. Maybe it was the death of my mother at an early age that changed my view of that, but these woods were my home. My base. As a child, it was the place that comforted me when my world was turned upside down. As an adult, these woods still comforted me when I had heartbreak or sadness or depression. They reminded me of who I was, of where I came from. They grounded me.

Suddenly, I heard a noise below the window. I looked down and saw Huckleberry there, eating away at the tin pans of burnt pie.

He was looking older and more haggard. His fur was wet with melted snow. He was shaking, and eating at the tin pans feverishly.

I watched him as he slopped away at them, standing still so as not to scare him. In a matter of moments, he had finished off both tins.

I expected him to dart away into the woods, the way he usually did. But he didn't. He looked up at me, and started whining.

It was a heartbreaking little whine.

Poor little Hucks.

Maybe he was ready. Maybe he was ready to trust me now.

I slowly turned the knob to the backdoor and opened it. I was met with a burst of frigid air.

"Come here, Huckleberry," I said, quietly. "Come inside, poochie."

He leaned back on his paws defensively, but stayed there. A good sign, I thought.

"Come here," I cooed again.

He started moving toward me. Slowly. Closer to the door.

I started smiling. Maybe he was finally going to trust me.

He got to the door threshold, and then placed a paw over it.

"It's okay," I said. "C'mon."

Suddenly, a gust of wind rushed through the kitchen, pushing the front door of the shop open, and slamming it shut with a loud crash.

I saw fear flash across Huckleberry's eyes. He backed away and took off, running back into the woods.

"Damn it," I muttered, watching him run.

But then he did something strange.

He didn't disappear. Not like he usually did, deep into the woods.

This time he sat there, waiting. Looking at me.

A crazy thought crossed my mind as I saw him gazing at me from the woods.

Did he want me to follow him?

I thought back to what Daniel had said about him. That he felt like the dog wanted him to follow him.

Was that true now? Did Huckleberry want more than just a few pieces of pie? Did he want something else?

It didn't take me too long to decide. I quickly took off my apron and went to the coat rack to grab my jacket. As I put it on, I went to the front of the shop to make sure there were no other customers. There weren't. I turned the sign around to say closed, and zipped up my down jacket.

When I went to the back door, Huckleberry was still in the same spot in the woods, still gazing at me.

I went out the door, closing it behind me. I walked down

the steps, and out into the woods, trudging through the thick snow as the skies above me turned red with the dying sun.

CHAPTER 15

He ran out ahead of me, but not so far that he lost me.

The deeper I walked into the woods, the more I felt like Huckleberry had a purpose, a reason for doing this.

He wasn't just a starved stray looking for a meal. There was more to it.

The snow was deep and I was breathing hard as I made my way through it. With each step, my foot would fall through several layers of the powdery white stuff. I almost stumbled a few times, falling down to my hips once, but I kept going.

Suddenly, I saw Huckleberry up ahead. He had stopped. He was waiting for me.

I tried to pick up the pace to get to him. He had started whining again.

"I'm coming," I yelled.

By the time I got to where he was, I was sucking in deep breaths of frosty air that stung my lungs.

"I'm right he—" I started saying, but then stopped mid-sentence.

Huckleberry was pacing around something. Something I

75

couldn't make out. Something covered by a layer of snow.

Then, my eyes fell on something that looked like a log sticking up out of the snow. A form that had previously just blended into the field of white.

I stood frozen for a moment, putting it together. Putting it together, but unable to process it.

Then, I understood.

I put my hand over my mouth and stifled the scream that traveled up my throat, looking for a way out.

The form in the snow. The outline. The pale purple color of it.

In the dying red light, I finally understood what it was.

A hand, sticking up from the blanket of rosy snow.

A frozen hand.

CHAPTER 16

I left Huckleberry barking around the hand and stumbled through the deep snow, back to the shop, back to a phone.

A feeling of absolute horror circulated through my body. I ran, falling into the brutally cold snow and getting back up again, and falling again and repeating the whole process like I was running from Jack Torrance in *The Shining*.

The sun had gone down, and the woods were falling into twilight, a gray dust settling over them.

It took me about five minutes of fighting through the snow to make it back to the shop. I rushed for the cell phone in my purse and called 9-1-1. I felt the snow melting on my jeans, and bleeding through to my skin. I couldn't stop shivering.

I tried to keep my voice steady as I talked to the operator.

"Is he alive?" she asked, her voice calm and steady.

"I don't know," I said.

But I was lying.

I did know. There was no other possibility.

Whoever that hand belonged to out there in the woods behind the pie shop was dead.

And had been for a while.

CHAPTER 17

Sheriff Trumbow told me to stay inside the shop while
they investigated the scene, so I did.

I could see their lights out in the woods and hear
the frightened barking of Huckleberry as several deputies
sectioned off the area.

I was still shivering. Daniel had put his coat around me,
and had poured me a shot of the Bourbon I kept in the
cupboard for the Bourbon Chess Pies I made in the
summertime.

He'd come at five instead of five thirty like he said he
would. He forgot about the revision in the plans. And when
he showed up, he was greeted with a row of flashing cop cars
parked outside my shop.

When I finished talking with them, telling the story of
how I was led to the body, I repeated the story to Daniel.
About how Huckleberry had come and eaten the pie scraps
and then waited out in the woods for me.

"It was just like you said, like he wanted me to follow
him," I said, trying to keep the shakiness out of my voice.
"Just like the other night. And then he led me to this
clearing, and that's where I saw…"

I trailed off.

He waited for me to continue. I took a deep breath.

"Where I saw the *hand*," I said, finishing the sentence.

"It's going to be okay, Cinnamon," Daniel said, placing the glass of bourbon in front of me. "Drink this."

I did as he said, the liquid feeling sharp at first, but then warm as it traveled down my throat.

He poured me another, but I let it sit on the kitchen island.

"What do you think happened?" I said. "Who is he and how did he end up out there? Do you think he got lost, or did he…. Was he…"

"Shhh," Daniel said. "Don't think about that right now. It's all going to be okay."

Suddenly, I heard the front door open in the dining room. I had the sign turned to closed, but hadn't locked the door. Whoever came in didn't seem to care about the sign.

"Cinnamon? Are you here?"

I let out a short sigh. It was John.

"Back here, John," I said.

"Cinnamon, I saw all those police cars out in front. Are you al—"

John entered the kitchen and saw me. And saw Daniel.

I saw a flash of anger cross his face. Anger that he tried to hide by averting his eyes.

"What's going on? Are you okay?" he asked solemnly.

I nodded and stood up.

"I'm sorry, I was just about to head over to your office. But something got in the way."

"But you're okay?" he said, giving Daniel a sharp and jealous look.

"I'm fine," I said. "It's just... I found something out in the woods back over there. I found a... it was a body in the snow."

"What?" John said, surprised. "How? What were you doing back—"

"She's already had to explain it to the cops several times," Daniel said before he could finish. "She should rest."

John's eyes narrowed with anger.

"And who the hell are you?" John said. "Clearly I haven't been made privy to that information yet."

"An old friend," Daniel said, standing up. "Now, I propose that we get you home Cinnamon. I'm sure the police will have more questions for you about what happened, but it can wait until the morning. You're in shock, and you need to go home and rest."

"Good idea," John said. "I'll take her."

"I can't yet," I said, shaking my head. "I told Warren I'd pick him up from the tavern in a little while."

"I'll take care of it," Daniel said.

"C'mon," John said, coming over to me. "Let's go."

"I can drive myself," I said. "I don't need to be carted around."

"No. You're in shock," Daniel said. "You shouldn't drive."

He looked at John.

"Make sure to get her home safe," Daniel said.

John didn't say anything. He just put his arms around

my shoulders in an awkward and uncomfortable way. He led me out through the dining room and through the front door.

Any other time, I might have protested more.

But a deep exhaustion had settled over me. Maybe it was the discovery in the woods, or the extreme highs and lows of the busy day, but I felt like a zombie emerging from the ground as I walked out of my pie shop.

John opened the door to his car and I got in, nearly falling asleep on my feet.

CHAPTER 18

O nce, when I was a teenager, I saw a pie eating contest at the Pohly County Fair where one of the participants ate too much pie and threw up all over the place before being rushed to the hospital.

There were rumors that a little girl riding the Ferris wheel found a regurgitated blueberry in her hair.

That was a hot mess.

But it was nothing compared to the kind of day I had had.

The only light at the end of the tunnel had been the fact that Daniel had been there for some of it.

I heard the front door slam just as I was dozing off to a rerun of *The Big Valley*, watching Victoria Barkley descend the stairs of her ranch mansion in an outrageous purple dress. I was lying in my room, wrapped in a pile of comforters and flannel sheets to get the cold out, but so far, it wasn't working.

John had tried to stay, but I told him I was tired and just needed some rest. He said he would check up on me in the morning and that he was glad I was okay. I thanked him, and then felt guilty about the whole thing.

I should have talked to him on the way over in the car about what I had decided, but it just never came up.

I sighed. There were some voices downstairs. Warren's, and then someone else's.

It must have been Daniel.

I suppressed a smile. That must have gone over well. After the second week of me moping around when Daniel left 17 years ago, Warren finally got it out of me what had happened. He told me that of course Daniel was probably going through a rough time, but that he should have returned my calls at least. Warren got pretty angry and threatened to go to California and find both Daniel and his father, and have a real talking to them. *Nobody treats my granddaughter like that!* I remember him saying. But I begged him to drop it, and he did.

Now, here Daniel was picking him up from the tavern. I was sure Daniel got an earful on the car ride over.

And maybe he did deserve it, in some ways.

I heard heavy, slow footsteps up the stairs, and then they stopped in front of my door. It creaked open, the hall light crept in across the wood floor.

"You awake, Cinny?" Warren whispered.

I sat up in bed and rubbed my eyes.

"I'm sorry I didn't pick you up," I said.

He came in and sat at the edge of the bed. He hadn't taken off his jacket and hat yet.

"Don't you worry about that," he said, patting my leg. "Your friend told me what happened."

I sighed and adjusted the pillows so I could sit up.

"Yeah," I said. "It's been a weird day."

"Do you want to talk about it?" he asked.

I pulled the covers around me tightly to lock out the cold.

"I didn't even see the body," I said. "Just a hand. It wasn't a big deal."

I was trying to brush it off, that same old defense mechanism kicking in. The one that tried to make others believe I was strong, to show that I couldn't be touched.

But Warren could see through all that. He always could. Like when I dyed my hair black in the seventh grade, or got a lip piercing a year later. Most parents would have freaked about those kinds of things. But Warren never did because he always saw those little acts for what they were—ways to feel like you had control over yourself and life when the truth was, you had none.

"Don't give me that," he said. "You're shook up. I can see that easy enough."

There was no use in trying to hide it. It'd just be a waste of time for both of us.

I rubbed my face, trying to erase the image of the frozen hand sticking up from the snow field that kept running through my head, but it was no use.

"I just keep wondering who he was," I said. "And how he ended up buried under the snow like that. It's just... it's a lonely way to go."

"Every way's a lonely way to go," Warren said. "In the end, we all come in this world alone, and we leave it alone."

"Yeah, but there's a difference between dying in your bed at home and being found in a snow drift."

Warren shrugged.

"His time was just up," he said. "One way or another. And there's nothing you could've done about that. Hell, nothing any of us could've done about it. He's just lucky you came along. He might have been there until the spring thaws."

Warren was right, but I was having a hard time hearing it.

I felt too close to all of it to see it from such a practical angle.

"But what do you think happened to him, Grandpa? How did he get back there, behind my shop?"

Warren stood up and leaned over, kissing the top of my head.

"Sometimes life throws us a curve ball like that. But don't let it get you down, darling. The police will do right by him," he said.

I nodded again and looked up at him. I flashed back to the time in the eighth grade when I fell off my bike riding home from school and scraped my knees to hell. He had that same look on his face then. He was concerned, but also confident that I was strong enough to get over it. He knew because my mother had raised me that way, and so had he. To be resilient and strong, even when things got rough or you hit a few bumps in the road.

That was the kind of person I was. He knew that, and seeing that he knew that sometimes gave me the strength to believe it was actually true.

"Now, do you need anything?" he asked. "Something to drink maybe? Some whiskey?"

"No," I said. "I'll be fine. Just some sleep."

He nodded and started walking out the door, but stopped as he got to the doorjamb.

"So he's come back, has he?" he asked.

It took me a moment to figure out what he was talking about, but then I realized.

"Like I said, it's been a weird day," I said.

"A lot of nerve he's got showing his face around here again after leaving the way he did," Warren said. "I let him know it, too."

"I wouldn't have expected anything less, Warren," I said.

I thought I saw him smile as he closed the door.

CHAPTER 19

The hand in the snow and the body that it belonged to wasn't the first dead body I'd ever seen.

But it's not like that thing ever got any easier. Especially when you weren't expecting it.

That night, I dreamed of that other time I saw someone dead. So many years ago, back through the haze of time and the fog of the dream world. Distorted and distant and empty.

I was out in the snow, with Huckleberry leading the way. The snow was rosy under the setting winter sun, the way it had been earlier. Huckleberry kept getting farther and farther ahead. I tried to keep up with him, but kept stumbling in the deep snow.

I looked up, and he was suddenly gone.

But there was something up ahead. Something I felt compelled I had to get to. Something that was calling my name.

I kept going and made it to a clearing, an area that must have been a meadow when it wasn't buried under winter snows.

She was standing there, waiting for me. Dressed in the

same outfit she had been when she went skiing that fateful morning, all those years ago.

She looked the same as she did then. With her short brunette hair pulled back into a pony tail, that same slightly flat nose that I saw when I looked in the mirror every morning. Those rosy cheeks and porcelain skin color that almost seemed to glow.

It was a strange sensation seeing her, realizing that she wasn't much older than I was now. That I was almost as old as she was when she died.

"It's been so hard to find you," I said.

Every step I took toward her, I seemed to sink deeper and deeper into the snow.

"Where've you been, Mom?" I asked.

She didn't respond. I stopped for a moment to catch my breath. I looked up at her. She was staring at me intently with a worried expression.

I followed her gaze, and gasped.

Blood was gushing from my chest, running down the side of my fleece jacket, staining my jeans black, dripping down onto the bright white snow.

The blood was spilling from a giant gash across my heart. A long, straight wound.

I looked back up at my mom, but she was gone.

I woke up crying in the cold winter morning.

It had been years since her skiing accident, but sometimes, the pain of her death still felt very fresh.

CHAPTER 20

When I got to the shop in the early-morning darkness, all the patrol cars were gone from the parking spaces in front. I went in, hung up my coat and scarf, and brewed up a pot of steaming coffee. Then, I went to the back window to look outside.

The empty pie tins were still there on the back porch, empty and sadly dilapidated in the cold snow.

I sighed, and looked out the window. I couldn't see much of anything. Just silhouettes of the trees swaying in the cold breeze, and a faint grayness at the edges of the sky.

I shivered.

They'd pulled a dead man out of those woods.

Who was he?

And how did he end up in the woods behind my shop?

Had he died of hypothermia? Was he homeless? Did he trip and fall and hit his head?

The strange feelings of the dreams came back to me. An unsettled feeling that I just couldn't shake. Like the way I sometimes felt before a late afternoon mountain thunderstorm during the summer.

"Get it together, Cinnamon," I said, looking at my

reflection in the window pane.

I was looking pale and shaky and tired and older than I would have liked.

I needed a vacation. I needed two tickets to Maui. I needed to feel the sun on my face, a warm breeze in my hair. I needed a break.

But I had to push those thoughts aside for now. I had to focus on getting through the season, and more than that, I had to focus on what would get me all of those things I wanted.

The Gingerbread Junction Competition.

I had to forget everything else and focus on what I was good at.

Which was building award-winning gingerbread houses, kicking ass, and taking names.

Making Bailey Jackson sorry she ever entered the contest.

Making her sorry she ever wronged me.

I looked at my reflection and changed my expression of worry into one of determination.

I nodded.

Then, I preheated the oven.

CHAPTER 21

Kara came over at around 9:30 a.m. with two peppermint mochas and a worried expression on her face.

By that time, I had baked the day's pies and already built the second and third story of the gingerbread house.

"Did you lose your phone or something?" she asked, stomping loudly into the kitchen.

"What?" I said.

"I'm just asking because I figured the only reason you wouldn't call your best friend about a dead body being found in the woods back there would be because you lost your phone. I mean, that's gotta be the only possible explanation, right? Some best friends might even think that excuse wasn't good enough, but you know, I'm a pretty forgiving person…"

I wiped the sweat from my brow that had accumulated from a long morning of opening and closing hot ovens and precariously balancing cookie panels on one another.

I looked up at Kara. She was pissed off. That much was obvious, but she was also worried.

"Word's gotten out?"

"Are you kidding?" she said, shoving the mocha into my hand. "It's the biggest news to hit Christmas River since that tourist accidently stepped out in front of a car two years ago and almost died."

"Small town living," I said.

"That's right. But I don't see why I had to find out about the dead body in your backyard from Moira Steward instead of you."

"He wasn't found in my backyard," I said, looking up. "And I didn't tell you because I didn't get a chance to. I barely made it home yesterday before I passed out from shock."

"Well, a text message would have sufficed," she said.

I took a sip of the mocha. It was rich and comforting, just like Kara knew it would be.

"Well, I'm sorry," I said, knowing that we wouldn't be able to move past it until she heard me say it. "Yesterday was just a... damn mess."

I sighed. That pissed-off expression on Kara's face disappeared, and only worry was left.

"And I just... I'm just trying to get myself back on track, you know what I mean? I can't think too much about the dead body or Bailey entering the contest, or telling John that it's never gonna work between us, because if I do, then I'm just going to freak out and turn into Cinnamon Peters' best impression of a beet salad," I said. "Which I can't let happen if we're going to be the Gingerbread Junction champions this weekend, all right?"

Kara was quiet a moment. I went back to placing a

gingerbread panel on the third story. Just as I set it where it needed to be, the cookie cracked in my stressed hands.

"Crap," I mumbled, throwing it aside.

"Wait a second," Kara said. "What was that you said about John?"

I smiled, amused.

Of course Kara would want to know that first, even before I told her more about the dead body.

"That's the least of my worries right now," I said.

"But something must have made you decide that—"

"Does anyone know whose dead body they found in my backyard?" I said, interrupting her. "Being that the whole town knows now?"

She hesitated for a moment and then shrugged.

"Not that I've heard," she said, taking a sip of her mocha. "Moira thinks it's a homeless man or a meth head who wandered out of the backwoods and froze to death. But you know Moira. She's been paranoid that she's gonna get robbed by some derelict character from those woods for years."

I started piping some decorative frosting onto the gingerbread windows. On a different day, that crack about Moira being a paranoid old lady might have made me laugh. But I wasn't in much of a mood for laughing this morning.

Kara placed her cup down on the kitchen island and came over to me, placing a hand on my shoulder.

"Are you sure you're okay?" she asked, looking at me with a worried look that made me feel like I was acting insane.

"Just dandy," I said.

Suddenly, I heard the front door bell jingle. A gust of wind blew back through the kitchen.

I placed the pastry bag down and wiped my hands off on my apron.

"I've got to help a customer," I said.

"Wait, Cin," Kara said. "They can wait a minute. Let's finish talking."

"I don't need to talk," I said. "I just need to forget."

"Cinnamon?" A man's voice said from the front.

Kara looked at me, raising an eyebrow.

Knowing right away that it wasn't John's voice.

"Yeah," I yelled. "I'm back here, Daniel."

Kara's eyebrows were just about through the roof by now.

I heard his boots against the tile floor, and then he came through the back door.

He took off his cowboy hat, and revealed his clean cut hair and beardless face that even after everything that had happened in the last 24 hours, still kind of made my breath catch in my throat.

I felt immediately better seeing him. It was a gut reaction that I had no control over.

"Well," Kara said, a dumbfounded look on her face. "I'll be. You've really been holding out on me, haven't you Cin?"

She went silent, even though she looked as though there were more things she wanted to say. She was giving Daniel the once over.

Daniel looked at her, and then back to me.

"You don't remember me at all, do you Daniel?" Kara said.

Daniel had that look on his face—the same one that he had when I called him by his name and drove away. That look people get when they realize that someone else knows them, but they don't know that someone. That unsettled look.

He cleared his throat.

"Uh, no. I'm sorry to say I don't."

"Don't take it personal," I said to Kara. "He didn't remember me either."

I looked at him and smiled, and he grinned sheepishly back.

"Kara," she said. "Kara Carmichael. U.S. Government and Politics? Ring a bell? You sat right next to me for half the year."

Daniel thought about it some, and then his eyes brightened.

"That's right," he said. "With old Mr. Stevenson. How could I forget?"

"Well, what happened to you?" Kara said. "You just disappeared our sophomore year without so much as a word, breaking Cin's heart without even calling."

If I wasn't already hot and sweaty from a morning of baking, I was now.

"She's just being dramatic," I said, shaking my head at him, and then shooting Kara a dirty look. "You didn't break my heart or anything."

"Now you're just being dishonest," Kara said, devilishly. "Remember? I was the one holding your hand while you cri—"

"I'm sorry to just barge in here like this," Daniel said,

interrupting Kara. I breathed a sigh of relief. "But I need to talk to you, Cinnamon, if you can spare a minute."

He looked at me intently, his eyes filled with some sort of urgency I didn't quite understand.

Kara threw her hands up.

"By all means," she said. "I was just gonna leave."

"No need for that," I said. "We'll step outside. If that's okay with you, Daniel? I could use the fresh air."

"Sure," he said.

I took off my apron, and he held the back door open for me.

We stood outside on the back steps where the empty pie tins remained wedged in the snow. We stood in the frosty air, looking out into the shadowy woods where ribbons of yellow tape were still strung across trees, marking the scene of where I had found the dead man.

CHAPTER 22

"That old timer's gotta be a handful," Daniel said.

I laughed, the frosty air feeling sharp and good in my lungs at the same time.

"Warren isn't the most forgiving person, I'm afraid," I said.

"Can't say that I don't deserve it, though," Daniel said. "If I hurt you then, you don't know how sorry I am. I was in a dark place for a while. There was no light for a long, long time after my brother…"

"You had a good reason for it," I said. "It's okay."

"It's not really," he said, sighing. "Your grandfather's right. I was a real jackass to you."

"Yep," I said. "Definitely sounds like Warren. Thanks for driving him home last night, by the way."

"Well, I'd say it was a pleasure, but I'd be telling lies just to get on your good side."

I smiled. Warren hadn't ever gotten along very well with Evan. I'd always thought it was just him that Warren didn't like, but maybe it was anybody I dated. Warren was like a father in many ways. No one was ever good enough for his little girl.

"So how are you dealing with all this?" Daniel asked, nodding out to the woods where one of the strips of yellow tape had broken loose and was flying like a flag in the wind.

"I'm fine," I said, feeling that rigid expression settle on my face. "I don't come across dead bodies every day, you know. But I'm all right."

"Are you sure?" Daniel asked.

I was sick of being asked that question.

"Of course."

"Because I've got a few things I've got to tell you about," he said. "And I want to make sure you're okay with this conversation before it begins."

"Tell me what?" I said, looking at him, confused.

He took a breath and leaned his foot against the wooden railing.

"The body you found out there?" he said.

I nodded.

"It was somebody you knew."

My mouth went dry. I felt the blood drain out of my face.

My mind raced with every possibility.

"His name was Mason Barstow," Daniel said, looking at me. "He was a judge for the Gingerbread Junction contest."

My jaw nearly came unhinged.

All that talk from Kara about the dead man probably being homeless or a druggie who wandered too far away from his meth lab made me think it could have been true.

But Mason Barstow? The Gingerbread Junction judge of almost ten years who spent most of the year in a vacation home in Arizona, who came back to Christmas River every year just to judge the contest, who wore designer clothes and jackets and stuck out like a sore thumb in a former logging town, who was stodgy and harsh, and who was particularly harsh when it came to my gingerbread houses, it seemed.

What was he doing in the woods back there?

Mason wasn't the type to take nature walks. He would've been too afraid the trails would scuff up his plush leather shoes.

So how did he end up there?

And how did he end up dead?

A sudden gust of wind ran through the pines and shook my back door wind chime. I shivered.

"Do you want to go inside?" Daniel asked.

I shook my head.

"It's better out here," I said.

"Well take my coat at least," he said, taking off the buffalo plaid coat and draping it over my arms. The second time in less than 24 hours.

I tried to say no, but it felt too nice to return it.

"Did you know him very well?" Daniel asked, shoving his hands in his jean pockets.

"No, I…" I stopped mid-sentence, struck by a thought.

Why was Daniel telling me this? How had he known about Mason Barstow?

It was something in his tone when he had asked me if I knew Mason well.

It wasn't just friendly concern. No. There was more to it.

"What's going on, Daniel?" I asked, looking back at him, catching those green eyes.

He pulled at a leather string on his cowboy hat, averting his eyes.

"We never got around to talking about what I did before I came back here," he said.

"No," I said. "We never did."

He took a breath.

"Well, Cinnamon, I'm a cop," he said. "Or, I was before I left my job."

A cop.

Things were beginning to make sense now. This wasn't just a friendly social call.

I cleared my throat and looked at him.

"And you're working with the local police on this? Is that right?"

He didn't meet my gaze.

"I should have told you earlier," he said. "Last night, Sheriff Trumbow asked me to help out with the investigation. I was a lieutenant back with the department in Fresno."

"I see," I said.

I wasn't sure why, but I immediately felt anger. For some reason, I felt deceived. It was innocent enough—given Daniel's background—that they'd ask him to help out. But I felt like somehow, he hadn't been honest with me. And I felt foolish thinking that he had stopped by to see how I was doing.

"Well, did Sheriff Trumbow say what happened to Mason?" I said, trying not to sound bitter.

"You're angry with me," Daniel said, cutting through my poor attempts at covering up my feelings.

"I'm not," I lied. "You're just trying to help out. Why would that make me angry?"

"Because you didn't know that about me, and you probably feel like I've been dishonest," he said. "But I haven't been dishonest about everything, Cinnamon. You know that, right?"

He leaned in toward me.

"Right?" he said, looking directly into my eyes.

I held his stare and then shrugged and looked away. Playing it cool, even though I definitely didn't feel that way.

In fact, when Daniel Brightman looked into my eyes like that, I felt the exact opposite of cool.

But I still wasn't sure if I could trust him.

I couldn't get hurt again.

"So how'd Mason end up out here?" I asked.

He didn't say anything for a moment.

And that look he had in his eyes faded, and once again, he was all business.

"First I wanted to ask what the nature of your relationship was to Mason Barstow," Daniel said. "It's just a routine question."

I ran a hand through my hair and sighed.

"He judges the… *judged* the Gingerbread Junction Competition. Has for about ten years now."

I leaned over the railing, looking out at the woods.

"So why'd you leave your job in Fresno?" I asked. "You know, just out of curiosity."

Daniel sighed.

"I'll tell you sometime but there are more important

matters at hand," he said. "How would you describe Mason?"

"Rich," I said, bluntly. "Stuffy and uptight, and aside from Gretchen O'Malley, my biggest hurdle at the competition."

Daniel was quiet for a moment, looking at me.

I sighed.

"I'm sorry," I said. "That was harsh. I know that. But I don't believe that just because someone dies we should lie about the kind of person they were. Ask anybody else in this town, and they'll tell you the same thing about Mason. He's the type that makes you think he was born with a red pen in his hand, ready to judge everybody and everything."

"I'm sure you're not wrong about him," Daniel said.

"Last year he told me that my gingerbread house was amateurish and could have been made by a ten-year-old."

"Ouch," Daniel said, smirking.

"I mean, it wasn't my best year. I'm the first to admit that. But I don't think it warranted that kind of criticism," I said.

"Sounds like a tool," he said.

"Well, you didn't hear that from me," I said.

"So you're saying he wasn't very well liked by others either?"

"I'm saying that some people probably liked him, but I wasn't one of them."

Daniel nodded and then looked like he was thinking about something.

"I appreciate your honesty," he said.

"Well, like I said. I'm not going to lie about him just

because he's not with us anymore."

"So why did he judge a contest like this?" Daniel asked. "I mean, it seems like a sentimental event. Why was he involved?"

"That contest is a big deal," I said. "It's a huge tourist attraction. It's gotten even bigger since you left. The town makes a lot of money off of it. I think Mason liked the feeling of power he got from it, from quashing people's dreams and calling them amateurish. Before he retired, he ran a string of successful restaurants, so he was qualified for it too."

"Do you know if Mason had enemies?" Daniel asked.

I thought about it for a minute.

And then thought about it some more when it struck me.

"What happened to him?" I said. "You haven't told me yet."

"It's just a routine question," Daniel said.

But I knew he was lying.

"Tell me, Daniel," I said, grabbing his arm lightly. "I've answered some of your questions. You answer this one for me."

"Okay," he said, tugging at the leather strap on his hat.

He paused. A cold breeze shook the wind chime behind us.

"Mason was… well, it looks like it was a homicide," he said, looking out into the woods. "We think he was murdered about a week ago."

I let go of his arm, and tried to keep my mouth from dropping.

"Murdered?" I said in disbelief.

"Murdered," he said. "And not 100 yards from your store, Cinnamon."

CHAPTER 23

"That's terribly unfortunate," John said, taking a small bite of his strawberry rhubarb pie.

Daniel had left after asking what felt like a never ending line of questions. When was the last time I saw Mason? How often did Mason come back to Christmas River? Did he have any friends or close acquaintances here?

Did I know why he would have been in the woods behind my shop?

Then, it felt like I had to answer those same questions all over again plus more about Daniel from Kara. It had been hard to get her out of the shop, despite the fact that I was sure customers were waiting for her back at her store. She was prodding me to spill my guts about what Daniel had told me, and how I had met him again, and where he had been all this time.

I didn't tell her much, saying we'd talk more later when we worked on the Western gingerbread mansion. She reluctantly agreed, but only after I promised her that I would tell her everything, and not to leave out a single detail.

It was noon, and John came in, as he always did at this time.

The day already seemed like it was one of the longest of my life.

When I saw him walk in and take his seat by the window, I knew I had to tell him.

I knew that I'd just have to suck it up and do it.

Regardless of what happened between me and Daniel, I knew that nothing would be happening between John and me. And he needed to know that.

But me, tough and invincible Cinnamon Peters, was having a hell of a time telling him.

But I didn't have to struggle with it too long.

"Listen, Cinnamon," John started. "I know that you're probably still in shock with all of this. But I feel like I've got to tell you something, and if I don't now, I'll probably never have the courage to."

"You really don't have to, Jo—"

Just then, the door opened and the jingle rang, and a frigid gust of wind came blowing through the dining room.

I glanced over.

"I'll be with you in just a mome—"

I stopped mid-sentence, all the breath escaping from my lungs in an instant.

"Take your time, honey," the woman said.

Not the woman. The witch. That would have been a more accurate description of her.

I stood paralyzed for a moment. Completely unable to move.

And sure that my heart would give out with such drama in the last 24 hours. Sure that a single heart wouldn't be able to handle all the surprises and shocks.

But my heart didn't give out. It kept beating. Beating hard and angry and furiously.

Bailey, with her bleach blond hair and trashy fur and feather fashion, stood in front of the door, a pleased, self-satisfied look plastered across her face.

I hadn't seen her in months. Hadn't spoken to her in two years.

So you can imagine my surprise that she was standing back in the shop where we used to work together. Where we'd laugh and tell one another stories to pass the time.

"Don't call me *honey*," I said, shooting her a bitter look.

"No need to be so touchy," she said. "I'm only trying to be friendly."

"What are you doing here, Bailey?" I said, doing my very best to keep my voice from shaking.

John looked back and forth between her and me, slightly dumbfounded.

He knew that my ex-husband had cheated on me, and that's why we had divorced. In a small town, it was hard to keep secrets like that, even when you wanted to.

But it was clear that he hadn't put two and two together yet. He still didn't know who this woman was.

"Well, I was in town and thought I'd stop by the old stomping grounds, you know?" she said.

She walked closer toward me, her heels clicking against the floor and all that cheap ugly jewelry she wore clinked and clanked together like she was a prisoner of Alcatraz.

"No," I said. "I don't know."

She sighed, like I was putting her out.

"Well, being as we're going to be competing against one another this weekend, I just wanted to extend a friendly handshake," she said. "Like, I wanted to bury the hatchet. I know we've had our differences, Cinnamon, but I'd be lying if I said I didn't miss you and you know, working here."

"That's not your hatchet to bury," I said, venomously.

"Okay," she said. "But you know that I'm sorry how everything turned out. Really I am. It was just bad timing. All of it."

I scoffed bitterly.

Bad timing? *Bad timing*. That's what she called it.

Homewrecking bitch.

I felt my cheeks grow red with fury.

"Listen, Bailey," I said, placing a hand on my hip and lowering my voice. "I don't want you coming in here. Ever. And if you don't leave now, I'm going to take that damn hatchet you want to bury so much, and you're not going to like what I'm going to do with it."

That kind of threat would reach most people. But Bailey wasn't most people.

"Aw," she said, placing a hand across her face. "And I was just about to order a slice of your famous Christmas River Cherry pie. Oh well."

She kept her hand on the side of her face. It took me a moment to realize what an unnatural gesture that was. But then I realized that there was a reason for it.

It was her left hand she was showing me.

I realized that there was a giant, sparkly rock on one of her fingers.

She watched as the realization hit me, relishing every second.

I was speechless for a moment. Breathless.

"Oh," she said, looking from me to the ring. "I forgot to tell you. I thought you'd want to know. Evan's proposed. We're getting married in the spring."

I felt my heart plunge to my feet, and could have sworn I heard the floor breaking as it crashed through the wooden boards on its journey down to a new level of hell.

"Congratulations," I said, sarcastically. "Just watch out for him. You know his history. Once a cheater, always a cheater. Now, if you would kindly get the hell out of my shop."

She didn't say anything in response. She knew that she didn't need to.

The ring said it all.

She started walking away, smiling cruelly.

"I'll see you this weekend, Bailey," I said to her back.

There was more I wanted to say about that, like how I was going to destroy her, but I couldn't say it without my voice trembling with rage.

She turned around as she pushed the door open and shrugged.

"Maybe," she said. "Maybe not."

She walked out, and I could hear her hoochie high heels clicking all the way down the block.

I hoped that they'd slip on some ice and send her crashing headfirst into the cold asphalt.

I sat down at one of the booths. John stood up, and came over.

"Are you okay, Cin?" he asked. "What was all that about? Who was that woman?"

He said it in that *doctory* kind of tone that just felt like he was prodding a hot poker into my wounds.

He was only trying to be nice, but I couldn't take nice at that moment.

"I can't talk right now, John," I said. "I need a minute. Can you give me some room, for the love of Christmas River?"

He was quiet, and then nodded as he looked at me sadly.

"Sure," he said, grabbing his beanie and tugging it on.

He walked out the door in a huff, and I watched as he crossed the street and turned up St. Nick Drive to his practice.

I knew I would be feeling bad about that later.

But right now, I couldn't feel any guilt.

All I could feel was a rush of red hot anger, that soon gave way to self-pity, that soon gave way to tortuous thoughts.

They were getting married.

The homewrecker could still throw a wrench into my life, even after setting fire to my world.

Now, she was dancing in the ashes.

It was just then that the front door jingled.

I wiped away the tear stains as best I could and looked up.

It was Sheriff Trumbow.

And I knew from the expression on his face, he wasn't there to eat pie.

CHAPTER 24

He left, asking if I had plans to leave Christmas River anytime soon.

That couldn't have been good.

The police had no doubts that Mason was murdered. There were several wounds in his chest that police believed had been made by a kitchen knife.

And apparently, they thought that I was a person of interest in the case. As made evident by Sheriff Trumbow's skeptical expression and his reluctance to answer any questions I asked him.

"It's still under investigation, Ma'am," he'd say.

I told him that Daniel had already asked me a million questions earlier, but that didn't seem to faze the sheriff. He wanted to hear my answers with his own ears, he said.

Maybe I should have held my tongue, but I told him outright that I had nothing to do with anything that might have happened to Mason. How could I have with the big competition coming up so soon?

Besides, hadn't I reported that a dog kept coming up to my back porch? Wouldn't I have known that it was Mason's dog if I had been the one to kill him?

Sheriff Trumbow didn't say much beyond that. He just asked me what I had been doing last week on Monday and Tuesday.

I said I was probably working late. That this entire month I'd been in my shop, working late. That he could check with Warren about that.

"So you've been on a losing streak at the Gingerbread Junction lately, haven't you?" the Sheriff asked toward the end of the questioning.

It was a loaded question, and I knew exactly where he was headed with it.

"I guess you could call it that," I said.

"I heard that Mason was a very harsh judge," Sheriff Trumbow asked, his small little hawk-like eyes looking at me like I was a mouse in a field below him. "I heard he was particularly selective when it came to your work."

"Listen, Sheriff," I said. "Mason Barstow and I weren't exactly buddy-buddy, but that doesn't mean a damn thing. Even I know that the gingerbread competition is just that— a competition. I take it seriously, but I'm not about to kill anyone over it."

The sheriff just stroked his uneven beard.

And then he asked if I was planning to stick around as he started heading for the door.

"I own my own business, Sheriff," I said. "I couldn't leave town this time of year even if I had the means to."

"Good," he said, plopping his hat on his head. It made him look like a sad version of Smokey the Bear. "I may have more questions for you soon."

"I'll be here," I said as he walked out of the kitchen and through the front door.

I'm sure that looked real good to the packed dining room of customers. A dead body found in my backyard, and then the sheriff waltzing out of my kitchen.

It seemed like there was even more people than usual today. Most likely here because of the news about Mason being found so close to here. People who were filled with morbid curiosity.

Sometimes, people were just the worst.

After the sheriff left, I went to the front of the house, filling up coffee mugs and making sure everyone was happy. Everyone was.

Everyone but me.

It was selfish. I knew that. Here I was, being on the verge of being accused of murder, and all I could think about was Bailey and Evan.

And that rock on her finger. A rock that was about twice as big as the small diamond ring he'd given me when we got engaged.

I'd be a complete liar if I didn't say that I wasn't ripped to shreds over it.

And it had happened just when things were getting better. Just when my life was starting to get back on track.

I went back to the kitchen where a fresh batch of gingerbread was rising in the oven.

And I started crying. Crying like I hadn't since I first found out about Evan and Bailey. Crying like the world was coming to an end. Crying like I was the only person left on earth.

Yeah. A real pillar of strength I was.

There was only one thing I could think of that might make me feel better.

I waited half an hour for the dining room to empty out and for the gingerbread to finish baking, then I pulled on my fur hooded coat.

I turned the front sign to say "closed" and I locked up the front door.

And I walked the three blocks through the bright streets that glowed with the Christmas spirit. The bright Christmas lights that no longer meant anything to me.

And I ended up at the humane society a couple of blocks away.

CHAPTER 25

It smelled like wet fur and muddied concrete at the humane society.

I asked Bridgette Andrews, who worked behind the counter and was the kid sister of Travis Andrews, a guy I went to high school with, if I could see the Australian Shepherd that was brought in the night before.

Daniel had said that Huckleberry was brought here for the time being. Since his owner was dead, and Mason didn't have any family, Daniel said that the dog would most likely go up for adoption once the police decided they didn't need him for the investigation anymore.

It was strange that Huckleberry had belonged to Mason. I didn't even know Mason had a dog. But maybe he had kept him at his house in Arizona most of the year.

But when I asked Bridgette if I could see the Aussie, she just shook her head.

"He's not here anymore," she said.

My heart sank. A cherry on top of the miserable day I'd been having.

"Where'd he go?"

"He was adopted out already."

"What? By who?"

"I can't tell you that," she said.

"Why not?"

"It's policy."

I shook my head.

What was I going to do? Track down whoever adopted Huckleberry and steal him from them?

I had come down here thinking I might adopt him. But now, all I wanted to do was say goodbye to the dog. To make sure he was safe and sound, and that he'd be treated right by his new owner.

Huckleberry. That sweet, poor creature that had been trying to draw attention to his owner's murder for over a week. That sweet dog that had brought a man I hadn't seen in 17 years to my doorstep.

That poor creature that had led me to his dead owner, buried in snow.

All I wanted to do was say goodbye to him.

But Bridgette Andrews was determined that I didn't get that chance.

She shook her head at me like I had bad credit and was asking for a loan.

I shook my head and left in a huff, wondering who would have scooped Huckleberry up so quickly and why the police would have just let him go right away.

It just wasn't my day. It seemed as though everything had been out of my control, and out of control.

But there was one thing I could control. One thing that I could do.

What people did throughout history anytime the world got too overwhelming.

Drink.

I walked along the cold streets. Some street vendors were setting up booths along the sidewalks. In all the "excitement" of the last two days, I had almost completely forgotten about the Christmas Parade and Festival. It always heralded the beginning of the mad-dash Christmas season, and always came right before The Gingerbread Junction Competition.

The thought of the impending barrage of Christmas spirit only made me pick up the pace to get to the Pine Needle Tavern quicker.

There was a glass of whiskey with my name on it waiting for me there.

CHAPTER 26

"Don't sweat it, Cinnamon," Harold, the bartender said, refilling my whiskey glass. "Anybody would have to be out of his mind to choose that Bailey over you."

I chomped down on a piece of ice I'd been clinking against my teeth.

"That's just something to say," I said, sighing and looking at the mirror behind the bar at my reflection. "Bailey's got some things going for her. She's attractive and young and smart."

"But she's missing the most important thing of all," Harold said.

"And what's that?"

He tapped his chest.

"A heart."

I smirked.

"That's something only a mother would say," I said. "You're getting soft, Harold."

He smiled, and then was called away by Phillip Cooke who was sitting at the other end of the bar, getting quietly drunk.

Phillip was, in impolite terms, the town drunk. But on nights like these, I understood him a little better.

Sometimes it was just easier to curl up with a bottle than it was to face life.

Tonight, I was giving in to that urge.

I took a sip of my whiskey and looked around at the bar. It was crowded tonight. Townes Van Zandt was playing loudly over the speakers.

Warren was there with a group of the old timers sitting at their usual table. I spent Whiskey number one with them, but didn't want to cramp Warren's style. They had old-man things to talk about, and I had some serious drinking to do, so I was spending whiskey number two at the bar.

There were a lot of locals in the bar, but there were also some unfamiliar faces. Some tourists in for the Christmas festivities, no doubt. This time of year, some would accidently wander into the Pine Needle Tavern. Most didn't last too long. They knew that they didn't belong here.

I played with my paper coaster and felt the warm tingle of the golden liquid crawling through me. It felt good, softening the blow of the dark thoughts that were creeping in. They got in, even in the noisy bar.

I was thinking about what Bailey had said before she left. When I had told her that I'd be seeing her at the competition this weekend, she had said *Maybe. Maybe not.*

What did she mean by that?

Probably nothing. She just had a flare for the dramatics. She just wanted to scare me with some impending threat of doom.

Sometimes I wondered how I could have been so absolutely wrong about someone. She'd worked in the shop for years, and I would have vouched for her without a moment's thought. I had thought of her as my friend.

But I'd been so oblivious to what was going on around me.

I suddenly wondered about Mason. If that's what happened to him. If he trusted someone, and ended up being wrong about them.

Dead wrong.

I wasn't any fan of Mason. That was well-documented. But maybe I'd only seen him in one kind of light. He couldn't have been all bad. And most likely, he probably didn't deserve to die alone in the woods, in the cold snows of December.

Sometimes, we were just victims of our own trusting natures.

I looked down at my drink and swirled it around before mumbling a little prayer for Mason.

Like I said. He couldn't have been all bad.

I hoped the gingerbread houses wherever he was were finally living up to his standards.

I downed the rest of my drink, feeling better as it traveled down my throat.

Harold poured me another before I could even ask.

He was a good bartender.

"Hard day, huh?" a voice said from behind me.

I looked up in the mirror and saw Daniel standing behind me.

And soon, I realized that he wasn't alone.

CHAPTER 27

"Huckleberry!" I said in a kind of girlish shriek that I seemed to have no control over when I saw that little black wet nose and those sorrowful little brown eyes.

I stood up off the bar stool and kneeled down on the ground, petting his now-shiny fur, and hugging him.

He wasn't completely buying into the idea and kept looking for a way to get away from the drunk woman's pets, but I didn't care. I was so glad to see him I didn't care how it looked to anybody.

I planted a kiss on his sweet, soft little head.

"So you're the one who beat me to the punch," I said, looking up at Daniel. "I swung by the humane society earlier, but he was gone by then."

"Well, I always kind of had the feeling that it was meant to be," Daniel said. "Ever since I saw him staring at me in the woods that night."

"There you go with fate again," I said, stroking Huck's fur some more.

Huckleberry was finally giving into my wild pets. He started licking the side of my face. It tickled and I started laughing.

"I thought you might want to see him again," Daniel said, kneeling down beside me.

He smelled good. Like he always seemed to. Like cedar.

"Listen," Harold said from behind the bar. "I don't want to be a buzz-kill, but we don't allow pets in here."

"Aw, c'mon, Harold," I said. "Make an exception, would you? This dog's been wandering around in the cold for over a week."

"Sorry, Cinnamon," he said. "Can't do it unless he's a guide dog. It's the code."

I sighed, and looked up at Daniel.

"I'll take my drink on the road, then," I said, standing up and taking the glass in my hand.

It wasn't really on the road, as I found out. More like through the bar, as I nearly inhaled it while grabbing my coat.

Daniel held onto my arm, steadying me as we walked out.

"Let me say goodbye to Warren first," I said.

"Let's hope he lets me walk out of here with you," Daniel said, smirking.

"Maybe you should wait for me outside," I said, winking.

He nodded and went out the front door, leading Huckleberry by his leash. I went over to Warren's table and asked Larry if Sheila could also give my grandpa a ride when she picked him up later that night. I told Warren I'd meet him back at the house.

"Don't think you're pulling one over on me," Warren said, raising his white eyebrows.

I smiled.

"Of course not," I said, putting on my coat.

"Then call me if you need anything. Even if it's something stupid."

Good old Warren.

I kissed him on top of his head and said goodbye.

Then I went out the front door.

But I didn't feel cold in the frosty air.

I wasn't cold at all.

CHAPTER 28

"I'm not usually like this," I said.

A light snow was falling, small crystalline flakes sailing through the dark night, gathering on the streets and sidewalks of downtown Christmas River, adding to the already thick snow drifts.

The red and green and white Christmas lights for the parade and festival had been strung up along street corners and alleyways, and they glowed in the darkness. A soft, icy wind blew through every once in a while, shaking them and casting shadows along the frozen streets.

Daniel and I were walking in no real direction. I was holding onto his arm. The cold air felt good against my rosy cheeks. Huckleberry was walking out in front of us, stopping every once and a while to sniff a bush or explore a patch of snow.

He seemed to be used to a leash, and seemed comfortable with us.

"I mean, don't get me wrong. I drink. But it's not too often that I *drink*."

Daniel smiled. It lit up my blurry night.

"You don't have to justify it to me," he said. "You saw

how drunk I was the other night."

"Yeah, but I don't want you thinking I'm a lush."

"That sounds like a word Warren would use."

"Hey, don't insult my grandfather like that."

"Then don't steal his old-man words."

I looked over at him, and we were both smiling.

"So tell me why you dove headfirst into a bottle of whiskey, Miss Peters."

I didn't answer for a little ways. The only sound was our footsteps disrupting the layers of snow.

"I prefer *Ms.*," I said.

"My apologies," he said. "*Ms.* Peters."

I sighed heavily.

"Because I found a dead body in my backyard," I said. "And the cops think… you, probably think, too… that I had something to do with it."

"Hey, I never said that."

"No," I said. "But that's probably why you're here. You're probably trying to catch me while I'm drunk. You think you can make me confess."

"I don't think anybody could get a confession out of you if you didn't want them to," Daniel said. "Even drunk."

"Is that a compliment or an insult?" I said.

"Do you really think I'd be here right now if I thought you could actually kill someone over a gingerbread contest?"

"I don't know," I said, shaking my head. "I don't know you that well. Maybe that's exactly what you would do. How should I know?"

Huckleberry pulled on the leash and Daniel followed,

breaking free from my grasp. He walked a few feet off the sidewalk, into a small clearing.

I followed him, digging my hands deep into my coat pockets. The chill was beginning to get to me.

He didn't say anything.

I stood next to him, looking out at the clearing that was Pioneer Park in the summertime, but was just a lifeless field of snow during the winter.

I watched Huckleberry and sighed.

"What are you doing back here, Daniel?" I asked. "You haven't really told me. I mean, not really."

"You know, I remember this park, now that I'm looking at it. There's a baseball diamond under all this snow, isn't there?"

"You're avoiding my question," I said.

He hesitated again.

"Let's just say something happened back in Fresno, and that all I could think about for months after was coming back to these mountains. All I wanted was to see snow again, and to feel clean air in my lungs. You know? All I wanted was to get back a piece of something I lost a long time ago."

He rubbed his neck, like it was sore.

"Is it helping?" I asked. "Being back here?"

I wanted to ask him more about what happened, but felt a wall when I started moving in that direction.

I got the feeling he didn't want to talk about it. Not yet, anyway.

"There are moments when it seems like it is," he said. "I see these Christmas lights and the snow coming down, and here I am walking down the street with a pretty girl in the middle of the night… everything back there seems very far away. But then other times…"

"Other times it's all right there," I said, finishing the sentence. "It's there, because it's part of you now. And there's no way to outrun it."

He looked over at me, and I thought I saw a hint of surprise in his eyes.

And then he nodded.

"I know a little something about moments like that," I said.

"I know," he said. "I can see it in you."

I thought of what he said the night I dropped him off at his home.

I don't want you to be sad anymore.

I realized I didn't want him to be sad anymore either.

"Copley intuition?" I asked.

"Is that why you're drinking tonight?" he asked. "I mean the real reason why."

"Finding a man you once knew dead in your backyard isn't enough to drive someone to drink?" I asked.

"Maybe for most people," Daniel said. "But you're tough. I don't think that'd rattle your cage so badly."

I shrugged.

"There's always a reason to drink if you're looking for one," I said. "In my case, I can blame it on an ex-husband and his lovely fiancée who just happened to be my bakery assistant in another lifetime."

He winced.

"That explains a lot," he said. "I don't blame you for falling into a bottle."

"If it were up to me, I'd spend a lot more time in a whiskey fog," I said. "But you know, I've got things to do, responsibilities and what have you."

"Plus, you're tough. You wouldn't fall off the tracks like that," he said. "I remember that about you."

I scoffed.

"You'd be surprised," I said. "You want to know a secret?"

"What's that?" he asked, leaning in closer to me.

"I'm not that tough," I whispered. "It's all a show."

He shook his head.

"You're not selling me on that," he said. "No. I know the truth, Cinnamon Peters. That you're nothing short of ruthless. Someone who's won as many Gingerbread Junction Competitions as you would have to be, wouldn't they? So don't try and convince me of something else. I know you, Cinnamon."

That made me smile.

And it suddenly made me feel a lot better.

That was something I remembered about Daniel.

He always had a way of making you feel special. Of making you feel like you were the only one in the world. Or at least the most important one.

Like he believed in you. Really believed in you.

"And what you said before? About you not knowing me? That's not true either," he said. "You know me."

"We'll see about that one," I said.

Huckleberry started leading us down a street that led away from the downtown area. There weren't many streetlights, but we kept going anyway. Christmas lights from the houses cast enough light to see by.

"So if I didn't kill Mason Barstow, who did?" I asked.

"Someone who didn't like him very much," Daniel said.

I laughed.

"Wow. And you made your way all the way up to lieutenant back in Fresno?"

"The department's an equal opportunity employer," he said.

We stopped for a moment. The street was getting too dark to see by. I could barely make out Huckleberry in front of us, and I could barely see Daniel's face.

"Should we turn around?" he asked.

"Sure," I said.

We swung around, me clinging onto his arm while we walked back toward the lights of town.

"But really," he said. "Do you have any idea who would have wanted him dead? Anyone else in the competition or in the town who didn't like him?"

I thought about it for a moment.

"Not anyone in particular," I said. "A lot of people disliked him. About the only person he did get along with was Gretchen O'Malley. He just thought she was some sort of artist with gingerbread. I never understood it. I guess they were cut from the same piece of mean and nasty cloth."

Daniel nodded.

"One time, he called her a Picasso with gingerbread."

Daniel laughed heartily.

"Sounds like a good name for a band, doesn't it?" he asked. "*Picasso with Gingerbread*. It's got a nice ring."

I thought back to him playing guitar that night under the stars.

"Do you still play?" I asked. "I remember you and that guitar back in high school. I never saw you without it slung over your shoulder."

"No, I haven't played for a while," he said. "It's just one of those things I kind of lost along the way. I miss it though."

"You should start back up," I said. "Teach me how to play. Remember how you promised to teach me that night? Now's your chance."

"Yeah, uh, sorry for being a few years late on that," he said.

"A few?" I said, looking up at him.

"Well, more than a few years. But, better late than never, right?"

We suddenly stopped walking, and I could have sworn the clouds up above broke for a moment, and a bright ray of winter moonlight fell on us. Light snowflakes floated magically through the air.

And in the white light of the moon, he looked the same. The same as that carefree teenager all those years ago, serenading me by the lake in the summertime.

"I've missed you, Cinnamon," he said.

"You're just saying that," I said as he wrapped his arms around my waist and pulled me close.

"Doesn't make it any less true."

He leaned over and his lips touched mine, and he kissed me tenderly, bringing me close to him in a passionate embrace. Making the cold night glow.

My heart pounded hard in my chest like it was a prisoner trying to get out of a burning jail cell.

He pulled away, smiling.

I felt my lips turn up. I was smiling too.

"Should you really have done that, Lieutenant Brightman?" I asked. "Kissing a murder suspect? Doesn't that violate some code of some sort?"

"You forget," he said as we started walking again. "I'm not a Lieutenant anymore. And even if I was, Cinnamon. It wouldn't matter."

We walked a little farther and ended up in front of his black pickup truck.

"You know, I really liked you," he said. "Sometimes, I've thought about what would have happened if I stayed behind."

I let out a sigh.

"I've thought of that before too," I said. "Would it have worked?"

"Maybe we'll get a chance to find out," he said, opening the truck door for me.

He drove me back home. It had stopped snowing.

As I got out of the car, he leaned over to say something.

"Do you forgive me yet?" he asked.

I made it look like I was thinking long and hard about it.

"Well, let's just say you're making some progress."

We made plans for him to stop by the shop the following day.

And I knew that the chills wouldn't come back that night.

CHAPTER 29

I woke up the next morning, feeling more awake and more alive than I had in a long time.

If I thought about it too much, I might have felt bad about the way I was feeling.

I might have felt bad that I was feeling so good with Mason dead. That I was feeling so good with me being a potential suspect in his murder.

But I was doing a pretty good job of not thinking about any of those things this morning.

I got dressed, shoveled the driveway, made coffee and breakfast for Warren and me, and got ready, thinking about Daniel Brightman's arm around my waist and his lips on mine.

That one image almost erased the fact that Bailey and Evan were getting married.

Almost.

But I promised myself I wouldn't dwell anymore on any of it until after the competition. Bailey was playing dirty. She had chosen to drop that bomb on me because she knew it would jar me.

I'd heard, through a friend who worked over at the

Chamber of Commerce, that she was planning on opening up her own bakery soon. She was just looking for publicity at this competition, no doubt, and was looking to upstage me.

But I wasn't going to let that happen.

I thought about what Daniel had said. That I was tough.

He was right.

I drove over to the shop in the dark wintry morning. Usually, it was silent and still and dead at this hour of pre-dawn. But today was the big Christmas parade. Burl Ives was already blaring from the speakers set up downtown as a flurry of behind-the-scenes parade people got the floats ready.

It was going to be a busy day at the shop.

The parade was always a high point in the tourist season. Because it took place right downtown, lots of locals and out-of-towner alike ended up wandering into my shop. I was going to be working hard, baking pies all day long to keep up with the stream of customers.

But I had some good thoughts to keep me warm.

I pulled up to the dark store and parked. I got out, and fished my keys out of my pocket, then opened the door.

Right away, I knew something was wrong.

A cold draft of wind hit me in the face, rather than the usual warm, cozy air that perpetually smelled of caramelized fruit fillings and buttery crust.

I stood in the doorway for a moment, frozen by a paralyzing fear.

I looked around the dark dining room. Nothing

appeared to be out of order. Everything was neat and clean, the way I left it last night before I locked the front door and closed up.

But I had a bad feeling in the pit of my stomach.

The blinds were moving with a draft that shouldn't have been blowing through.

And whatever was wrong had happened in the kitchen.

I thought about calling the police or calling Daniel. But an uncontrollable need to know gripped me. That, and the fact that it was my shop, and I wasn't going to wait 15 minutes before I found out what was wrong.

I walked cautiously across the tile floor, leaving the front door open behind me in case I needed to get out quick.

I walked behind the counter, and then took a deep breath.

I went through the swinging door to the back, my throat dry like I'd swallowed a handful of sand.

My eyes scanned the dark kitchen. I flipped on the light switch.

I didn't see it right away. But when my eyes drifted over to the far right corner of the kitchen and saw the crumbled mess in the corner, I nearly fell apart, right then and there.

I dropped my bag and ran over to it, no longer caring if the burglar was still in the shop.

No longer caring that a window was broken, with a gaping hole chilling up the kitchen.

All I could see were the ruins in the corner.

I screamed in a kind of mad, crazed anger. I felt like I might blow my top, like my anger might shoot upwards and break my skull into a thousand pieces as the rage looked for an escape from this pent-up body.

My dreams of winning this year's Gingerbread Junction Competition were lying in a crumbled, mangled heap on the kitchen floor.

CHAPTER 30

"So you locked up the store about 6 p.m. last night? Is that right?"

I nodded solemnly.

We were standing in the kitchen, the bright and cheerful sounds of the Christmas parade bleeding through the big hole in the back porch window.

Sheriff Trumbow looked tired. A murder and break-in in the span of 48 hours would do that to a man. Especially a man that normally doesn't do much more than push paper from one side of his desk to the other.

"Any idea who would have done this?" the sheriff asked.

I had plenty of ideas. Plenty.

But it was just a matter of telling the sheriff without sounding like a jealous ex-wife.

"You know how the Junction gets," I said. "But this has never happened before."

I rubbed my face.

"The only difference this year, that I can think of, is that Bailey's entered the contest."

I glanced at the sheriff. He lifted his eyebrows at me.

He didn't know all the details, but he knew enough to

know that Bailey and I hated each other.

"Do you think she was capable of doing this?" he asked.

I shrugged.

"Honestly, I can't answer that question objectively," I said.

He rubbed his red face.

The back door opened, and a deputy who had been out on the porch looking at the broken window came in, holding something in his gloved hands.

"Did you leave this outside, Ma'am?" he asked, holding up something shiny.

I squinted at it, the light catching the steel and blinding me for a moment.

Then, with horror, I realized what it was.

The knife didn't belong to me.

"Where was that?" I asked.

"In one of the empty pie tins on your porch out here," he said. "Is it yours?"

I shook my head, feeling like I had just stumbled into some quicksand.

"Burglar must have left it," I said.

What was *that* doing on my porch?

How on earth did it get there?

I glanced over at the knife block on the counter. All but one was there, and that one was up in the front case.

Plus, I didn't recognize this knife.

The deputy looked at me hard for a moment and then placed the mystery knife into a bag.

I had a bad feeling about that. A real bad feeling.

"A lot of strange things going on in and around your shop lately, Miss Peters," the sheriff said.

"Don't I know it," I said, trying to sound calm. "What about this break-in? What can you do, Sheriff?"

He put his notepad away into his top pocket and readjusted his *Smokey the Bear* forest ranger hat atop of his balding head.

"We'll do what we can," he said. "We'll test the doorknob for fingerprints, and see about what Deputy Greene found out there. Hopefully, we'll find something."

"I don't suppose the penalties for destroying a gingerbread house are too severe?" I asked, feeling a drop of sweat form on the side of my temple.

"Well, no," he said. "But breaking and entering is serious."

I nodded.

"That is, if anyone actually did break in and enter," he said, clearing his throat.

I was about to ask him something else, but then realized I didn't understand what he was talking about.

"What do you mean? Of course someone broke in. How do you think that window was broken?" I said.

He stuck out his upper lip, like he didn't believe what I was saying.

"We just have to wait and see," he said.

He tipped his hat and then him and his deputy went out the front door, leaving me with a mess of glass and broken gingerbread on my floor, and an uneasy feeling in my gut.

That last thing he said just wasn't sitting well.

What was that supposed to mean?

Did the sheriff think I had something to do with the break-in?

Did he think I would have done that to my own shop? That I would self-sabotage myself in some sort of elaborate scheme?

The front door bell jingled, and I realized that I needed to get to work, otherwise one of the biggest money-making days of the year would be ruined, just the way the gingerbread house had been.

And I couldn't be a victim twice over. Not when there was something I could do about it.

CHAPTER 31

"I'm going to murder that…"

I thought I could see steam coming out of Kara's ears as she tried to find the right word to describe the soulless person who would destroy a work of art with such malicious hatred.

She struggled for the word, and finally just settled on looking down at the crumbly cookie frosting mess at our feet.

Eventually, we would have to clean it up. But not yet. It was still just too painful.

I was rolling out pie crust when Kara came in. I had phoned her earlier to let her know what happened. She was at the shop about five seconds flat after that. I didn't want to think about how she got here through all the parade traffic outside. I could just imagine her weaving her car around the Christmas River High School marching band and the news channel weatherman's float while honking and yelling at them to get out of her way.

"I mean, is she insane?" Kara said, rubbing her temples. "Doesn't she know that by doing this, she's put her life in danger?"

"Best not to even joke about those things," I said. "Given what happened to Mason."

Kara crossed her arms.

"Who said I was joking?" she said. "And Mason's got nothing to do with this."

"I'm not so sure," I said. "I don't know what in the hell's been going on lately. But it all seems to be happening around my shop. I've been thinking, and I'm not sure that it's all just coincidence."

Kara looked up at me, catching my eyes.

"There's something else I haven't told you," I said quietly.

"What?" she said.

"The sheriff found something else when he was here," I said. "Something out on the porch. Somebody left a knife out there."

"A knife?" Kara asked, saying the words so quietly, it was like she was lip syncing them.

"I'm really worried, Kara," I said. "I feel like something's going on and I don't have a clue what it is."

"It's gotta be Bailey," Kara said. "She's messing with you. But do you think she killed…"

Suddenly, there was loud yelling and hollering coming from outside. The parade was turning down Main Street. Santa's float couldn't have been too far behind given the loud screaming going on.

"No," I said, shaking my head. "Bailey's stupid and she's a homewrecker, but a murderer? I doubt she'd have the guts for that."

Kara nodded.

"But I wouldn't put it past her to… arrange something," I said.

"I wouldn't either," Kara said.

"But I just don't see the angle," I said. "I don't know what killing Mason would have gotten her."

I shook my head.

"And why is she doing this all of a sudden? She's getting married to Evan for goodness' sake. She's got the ring. She's got everything. Why all this now? I haven't even seen either her or Evan in months."

Kara shrugged.

"Who knows why crazy bitches do what they do," she said. "All I know is that we're screwed."

I sighed. She was right. There was no way we had enough time to make another gingerbread mansion.

The contest was lost before it had even started.

All my dreams of bright, sunny skies and warm sandy beaches and tanning oil lay somewhere among the broken cookie paneling of the gingerbread house on the floor.

And I couldn't even grieve for it properly. I had too much work to do in the kitchen for the hordes of tourists who would be coming into the shop after the parade finished.

Kara saw the look in my eye. That tired, exhausted, stressed-out as a one-legged table kind of look.

"Listen," she said. "I should get back to my store, too. But I'll be back tonight with some wine and we can plan on how we're gonna exact our revenge, all right?"

I nodded, wiping away a drop of sweat that was running down my temple.

"There's a lot going on that I don't understand," Kara said. "But there is one thing I know, Cin. She's going to be sorry. Very, very sorry when we get through with her."

I tried to smile, but no matter how much I willed myself to, I couldn't do it.

"I'm sorry, Kara," I said. "I'm sorry if she did this to get back at me. Going after the gingerbread house is a low blow. She shouldn't have included you in her warpath."

Kara half-smiled.

"She involved me the day she betrayed you, Cin," Kara said. "And the bitch doesn't even know the meaning of warpath. Wait until she sees what we've got in store for her."

Kara left, and I could hear the screaming of the crowd as Santa Claus's float meandered down the street.

The sharp noise grated on me like I was a chunk of hard cheese.

Which was exactly how I felt. Cold and hard, and completely devoid of holiday cheer.

CHAPTER 32

I felt like I could have slept for a decade.

The tourists were coming in and out of the shop like there was a food shortage in town, and my place was the only one with supplies.

I was running back and forth between the front counter and the kitchen, bringing out fresh pies and taking money and doing loads of dishes. It was utter madness, and it reminded me that I really needed to get someone to take Bailey's place. It had been far too long since I had help at the shop, and I kicked myself for getting into this situation again. Owning my own pie shop was a dream fulfilled, but I didn't bank on playing cashier or waitress when I had set up this place.

Finally, around late afternoon, the tourists were steadily filtering out, which was a good thing because I was nearly out of pies and even ingredients to make pies.

On the bright side, I had made a lot of money for the day. I tried to focus on that as I loaded up the dishwasher with another batch of plates.

I heard the front door jingle and washed my hands before going out to meet the customer.

"What can I get you to—"

I stopped mid-sentence.

"I'll take a piece of the blueberry," the woman said, pointing at the glass, her big, clunky wedding ring catching the light.

"Well," I said. "This season's full of surprises. I didn't ever expect to see you here, Gretchen."

Her graying hair was puffed out from the winds outside, and she had on her trademark big fur coat. The muted light of late afternoon fell harshly on her wrinkled face. She looked like a mummy who was in need of a drink of water.

But there was something different about her than when I normally saw her from across the Christmas River auditorium, standing in front of her gingerbread house.

That arrogant look that was normally on her face was no longer there. She actually looked almost normal. Not the archnemesis enemy she'd been all these years during the competition.

"I was in the neighborhood," she said. "And I just wanted to see how you're doing. I heard about… Mason."

I handed her a slice of pie, raising my eyebrows.

I looked at her hard for a moment.

Gretchen, in all the time I had known her, had never so much asked me how I was doing in casual conversation.

Now, after my gingerbread house was destroyed by an unknown assailant, she was here, snooping around.

Was this her way of gloating? Had she been the one to ruin my hopes of ringing in the New Year on a tropical island?

"I'm fine," I said. "As for Mason, he's most definitely not, as you've probably heard."

She winced. The first time I had ever seen any form of emotion on her face other than arrogance or jealousy when I took the competition from her.

I was speechless for a moment. I didn't expect the news about Mason to have that effect on her.

I mean, Mason loved her creations. *Loved* them. But Gretchen was such a snob that I never got the feeling she looked at Mason as anything other than a minion of sorts. He was someone she could depend on at the competition to give her the win. This perhaps was why she was lamenting his death.

She knew with Mason gone, she couldn't count on anything.

Not that it mattered, though. With me out of the picture, she'd take it, easy. I didn't give Bailey a chance against the experienced Gretchen O'Malley.

"It's just so shocking, isn't it?" she said. "I just can't believe that could happen in a town like Christmas River. I thought this was a safe place."

"Well, it's always a safe place until it isn't," I said.

There was a moment of silence. I suddenly got the impression Gretchen was here for something else. To ask me something.

She looked at me for a moment, and then cleared her throat.

"Do you think he suffered?" she asked.

She said it with a sincerity that took me by surprise.

She said it the way you would ask after a friend.

I hadn't realized that Gretchen O'Malley was human.

But maybe I had been wrong.

"I wouldn't know," I said. "By the time I found him… it was hard to tell. But I'm sorry if the two of you were close."

"No, no. We weren't," she said. "It's just… he was such a mainstay at the competition every year. An institution to himself. It's a shame he perished like that."

Leave it to Gretchen to call Mason Barstow an "institution." And to make it sound like he was a bag of lettuce left too long out on the counter.

She placed the untouched pie plate back on the glass case, lightly sliding it toward me.

"See you tomorrow at the competition?" she said. "The beat must go on, right?"

I let out a troubled sigh.

I was just about to tell her about what happened, about my gingerbread house being destroyed when I stopped myself.

The beat must go on.

That phrase seemed to resonate with me in that moment. It rang true.

She was right.

Even in the face of sabotage, I wasn't going to give up on the competition. I wasn't going to let anyone stop me with gutter tactics.

It wasn't in my nature to quit. To let anyone make me quit.

I was going to compete. Even if all I showed up with was a store-bought gingerbread kit and some gumdrops.

Because winning wasn't the point anymore.

The point was showing up, showing Bailey that she hadn't beaten me. That she couldn't break my spirit. No matter what dirt she flung my way, I would stand tall and wouldn't give up.

"Yeah, of course," I said. "See you there."

The corners of Gretchen's mouth almost turned up into a muted smile. She then walked out of the shop, the door slamming behind her. I saw her get into the passenger side of a car waiting out in front where I could make out the silhouette of her husband in the driver's seat.

I watched them pull away down Main Street, still strewn with parade streamers and horse droppings.

I turned the front sign over to "closed" and locked the front door.

Then, I went into the back and preheated the oven. I sent a text message to Kara to come over if she could. As I started mixing the ingredients for gingerbread, I thought about how odd things turned out sometimes.

That my archnemesis, Gretchen O'Malley, would give me the exact inspiration I needed to carry on in the competition.

That she would come through in my hour of need.

Yep. It had been a bizarre week. That was for sure.

CHAPTER 33

I was exhausted, but I was determined. And determination can take you through just about anything.

But I wasn't so exhausted that I didn't notice that Daniel hadn't stopped by, like he said he was going to the night before.

I tried calling him, but it just went to his voicemail. I sent him text messages, but heard nothing back.

As we rolled out sheet after sheet of gingerbread cookie dough, Kara noticed me stealing glances at the kitchen door from time to time. I told her about Daniel, and how he was supposed to be coming but hadn't shown up yet.

"Be careful, Cin," she said. "You might not, but I remember how devastated you were when he left the first time."

"The first time? Doesn't that imply that there's going to be a second?" I asked.

"I'm just saying," she said.

I didn't respond. I didn't feel like fighting her on this. I was too tired.

But I would have been lying if I said that the thought hadn't crossed my mind, too.

I couldn't let that happen to me. Not again. He seemed different than he had been all those years ago. More mature. But I knew that when it came down to it, most of us never changed.

Deep down, we were all the same as we had been in high school.

Like Evan, for example. During senior year, I found out that Evan had made out with another girl at a Christmas party I didn't go to because I'd come down with the flu.

I had been angry, but he had apologized to me, and like a fool, I had accepted it and kept dating him.

Years later, it happened again, only much worse. And this time, there was no real apology. And it wouldn't have mattered anyway. I wouldn't have taken him back.

But he was the same person he was back in high school. I had just been too blind to see it.

Maybe Daniel was the same he'd been in high school. Someone who blew out of town without so much as a word, not caring about the sadness he left in his wake.

"I just don't want you to get hurt," Kara said. "You deserve a good man. A man who'll treat you like the queen you are. You've had enough duds in your life."

I scooped some frosting into a pastry bag.

"I won't get hurt," I said.

But I knew that I couldn't control that. Not really.

We spent the rest of the night up to our arms in gingerbread dough and frosting and marzipan and candy decorations. The wind howled outside as a blizzard descended upon Christmas River, burying everything under a fresh, three-foot coat of snow.

And as the dark sky gave way to the grey fingers of dawn, we finally placed the final candy decoration on the gingerbread house.

Kara and I looked terrible. Hair plastered to our faces with sweat. Bloodshot eyes. Melted makeup.

But we had finished.

We had made the gingerbread house in record time.

And suddenly I felt sure that there was no way in hell that Bailey was going to beat us.

CHAPTER 34

We had a few hours before the competition started over at the auditorium.

Kara and I decided to take turns guarding our Western gingerbread mansion until we could transport it. She took the first shift while I went home to clean-up.

As I was leaving out the front of the shop, I noticed something taped to the door window.

I dusted the snow off of it, and found my name scrawled across the front of a card.

Scrawled in familiar handwriting.

For a moment, I hesitated in pulling it off from the window.

I knew who it was from, and I wondered whether or not I should open that can of worms. Especially with the competition in only a few short hours.

I wondered how long it had been taped to the door. It hadn't been there when I had unlocked the door for Kara the night before. Sometime during the big blizzard, he had come by and placed it there.

I took it down and held it between the thumb and fingers of my mitten as I walked to my car, buried in snow.

After I scraped off the windshield and pushed the snow off the hood, I got in the cold car, took off my mittens, and against my better judgment, I opened the letter.

"Dear Cinnamon,

There's something I have 2 talk to you about. I will b at the gingerbread competition. Please take a moment for me. I've needed to talk to you for a long while now.

Good luck, Cin.

Cheers."

I read the note over and over. Astonished at the arrogance in it.

Not even signing his name, assuming that I already knew who the handwriting belonged to, which I did, but still.

It was unbelievable.

Especially because I already knew what he wanted to tell me.

Evan wanted to tell me that he was getting married.

He must not have realized that Bailey already beat him to the punch.

"Un-f-ing-believable," I said, crumpling up the paper and throwing it in the back of the car before starting it up and pulling out in four-wheel drive.

I wouldn't have any time for Evan today.

Or ever, for that matter.

CHAPTER 35

I went home, took a long hot shower, drank a few cups of coffee, and then got dressed. I went with a simple and elegant black turtleneck, a suede skirt, and my lucky red cowboy boots.

When I came downstairs, Warren had a big plate of over-easy eggs, bacon, and pancakes waiting for me.

It must have been the exhaustion, but I felt my eyes grow wet with tears.

"I figured Wheaties wouldn't cut it," Warren said. "Go get 'em today, kiddo."

I wiped away the tears before they could slide down my cheeks and gave him a big hug.

Even when it felt like every man on earth had abandoned me, I knew it wasn't true.

I always had one man who would stand by me and support me in anything and everything I did.

"You shouldn't have troubled yourself, old man," I said, pulling away from him.

His eyes were glassy, too.

"Pish posh," he said, waving his hand.

He was too good.

I sat down and scarfed down the entire plate while he sat across from me drinking coffee and reading the paper.

I finished and then went to the door to pull on my jacket and scarf.

As I opened the door to leave I blew him a kiss and said goodbye.

"I'll start packing my bags for Hawaii," he said.

I laughed.

"I'll see you when I get back," I said.

"See ya, champ," he said.

I closed the door. Even though I hadn't slept in what felt like days, I felt a renewed spark of energy.

Like I could conquer the world.

CHAPTER 36

The Gingerbread Junction Competition was more crowded than I had ever seen it before.

All the usual competitors were there, including a few new ones, but there seemed to be a never-ending stream of spectators flooding the auditorium.

On top of that, word had gotten out to local news organizations in the state about Mason's mysterious death and how the town was continuing on with the competition, mostly fueled by a desire to make money off of the tourists. The place was crawling with camera crews and news reporters.

I felt thankful that the police hadn't given them my name or mentioned that the body had been found in the woods directly behind my shop.

I wouldn't have been able to deal with their questions on top of everything else.

There were police there, too. Sheriff Trumbow was in one corner, surveying everything.

I noticed that he was looking at me often. I wondered what that meant. I didn't think it could have meant anything too good.

Maybe I would have been more worried if it weren't for everything else that was going on.

And anyway, I was past the point of caring. Sheriff Trumbow seemed to think that I was guilty of something. But it no longer seemed to matter.

Once I had won, he could grill me all he liked.

Kara and I carefully carried our masterpiece into the crowded room, people splitting like the red sea in front of us as they eyed our creation.

It may have been the exhaustion bleeding into my thoughts, but this new gingerbread house that we had created was almost better than the one that had been destroyed. The decorations were better, the candy sheriff's and marzipan horses and drinking wells and snow-covered willow trees were more realistic. The house was better constructed and better decorated; looking like Hansel and Gretel had wandered into *The Big Valley*.

It may have been the best gingerbread house we had ever made.

And whether we won didn't even really matter anymore. The tropical vacation would be nice, but that was no longer the point.

The point was that we had already won on a more important and meaningful level than any judge could give us.

CHAPTER 37

I saw Bailey and her sister across the room. Bailey's stringy, bleach blond hair was elegantly hanging in a loose pony tail. She was wearing high heel boots and a tight-fitting sweater with long feather earrings.

She was standing by her cookie house. The one she had made with her sister.

It was better than I thought it would be. Much better.

"I'm going over there," Kara said, once we had draped the table with a cowboy-inspired table cloth and arranged the gingerbread house nicely on top of it. "Remember what I said, about her paying for what she did? Well, it's time to go collect."

"No," I said, stopping Kara. "I'll go. You stay out of this. It's between me and her."

"No," Kara said. "It's between her and us. Now let me—"

"Man the fort here," I said. "Let me deal with her."

Kara let out a long frustrated sigh.

"Fine," she said. "But I'm you're wing man, wing woman. Whatever. Get me if you need help."

"I will," I said.

"Because you know I would just love to—"

"Got it," I said.

I took a deep breath and threaded my way through the crowd over to her table.

I was going over there to show her that I was here. That I hadn't been beaten. That I wasn't going to let her break me.

And, I was going over to do something else. Something that I knew I needed to do. Not so much for her, but for me.

When I showed up in front of her table, she didn't say anything for a moment. She just stared at me. Speechless.

But then, the shock that was plastered on her face quickly disappeared as she scrambled for something to say.

I beat her to it.

"Good to see you here, Bailey," I said. "Good luck to you."

It took her a moment to respond. I could tell by the twitching in her face that she wasn't sure what to say. She wasn't sure if I was being sincere, or if I was being sarcastic.

I glanced at her house.

It was ornately decorated and looked to be quite well-made.

And there was something familiar about it, too.

There were small marzipan horses and even a sheriff.

The sign next to her house said *A Western Christmas*.

I looked up at her, and smiled. Knowing I had caught her.

I had a story I could go to the police with now. Something real.

What were the chances that she'd do exactly the same

decorations as Kara and me? Bailey didn't know what our theme was this year. It wasn't damning evidence, but it would give the sheriff a reason to look at Bailey more closely for the break-in, and who knew… maybe Mason's murder, too.

"I guess you didn't expect to see me here," I said. "You thought you'd taken care of me, isn't that right?"

"What are you talking about?" she said, looking around the room, her eyes seeming to dance with denial.

"I'm not that easy to get rid of, I'm afraid," I said to her. "Something you didn't count on."

"Get away from my table," she finally said, looking at me with hateful eyes that would have given a weaker person a serious case of chills.

But I wasn't weak anymore. I was strong. And she no longer could get to me. Not ever again.

I started walking away but then stopped, remembering something. I turned back. She was watching me.

"I almost forgot," I said. "I came over here to congratulate you."

"What?" she said, venom oozing from her voice.

"On getting engaged. I mean it. Congratulations. I wish both of you all the happiness in the world."

I may have hated Bailey, but as I said the words, I knew that I was being sincere.

I did mean it. I wished them all the best.

They deserved one another.

It wasn't so much about them anymore and what they had done to me. It was about me moving on. It was about forgiving them for what they had done. Not because they deserved it, but because I did. I deserved to be happy and to be clean of all the ugliness that their betrayal had brought into my life.

I deserved a fresh start.

I walked away from Bailey's table, feeling her dagger eyes on me the entire way across the room.

I smiled at Kara as I took my place behind our table.

"Did you give her hell?" Kara asked.

"I didn't need to," I said.

CHAPTER 38

Kara and I manned our station as townsfolk and tourists alike came strolling by, ogling our mansion. It felt good. The house seemed to go over well with just about everyone. But it didn't really matter what they thought of it.

All that mattered was what the judges thought.

I watched the three of them, dressed up in official jackets like it was a dog show, make the rounds to all the tables. I knew two of the judges—Adam Bybee, a retired baker, and Shanna Wellington, a pastry chef from Portland. The other one I didn't know. He was filling in for Mason, and I had no idea what he was looking for in our gingerbread houses.

I watched as they went over to Gretchen's table. She was back in fine form, that familiar smug look on her face. Her husband was standing by her, the two of them the picture of dysfunction.

I hadn't had a chance to see what she'd come up with this year.

But despite Gretchen being my competition archnemesis, my views of her had changed a little since the day before. I actually saw some feeling in her, some humanity.

163

And she had been the reason Kara and I were here today with our completed mansion.

Maybe she wasn't as bad as I had initially thought.

"All right, Cin, you ready for this?" Kara asked me.

The judges were just a few houses down from ours.

"Damn right I am," I said.

I looked at her, and squeezed her shoulder.

And I was overcome with a feeling of gratitude for the people I had in my life.

In addition to Warren, Kara was always there for me, too. She'd stuck by me and been there to pick up the pieces when things went sour.

When others left, she was always there.

She was a true friend, and I was grateful for her.

***

As the judges started marking down things on their clipboards and eyeing the construction of our Western gingerbread mansion with serious faces, I glanced across the room, and suddenly noticed someone looking at me.

Staring at me.

He looked older since the last time I saw him. Grayer in the face, and a few strands of gray muddled his usually chestnut-brown hair color. His hair, too, was longer. Shaggy and almost sloppy-looking. He seemed to be a little thinner than he used to be, too. But he still wore that old stupid beige barn coat and a pair of snow boots that he trudged around in on the weekends.

I tried to ignore Evan, focusing as best I could on the

judge's questions. But it was hard. My eyes would just drift in that direction without me wanting them to.

I just wished that he'd go away and stop haunting me during the most important moment of the competition.

I glanced over at Bailey's table and realized we were in a triangle stare-down of sorts. She was looking at Evan, he was looking at me, and I was looking at her.

She suddenly noticed me and whispered something to her sister. Then she left her table and disappeared into the crowd.

"How long did this take you gals to make?" Shanna Wellington asked us, writing something down on her clipboard.

"About one night," Kara said.

"One night?" Shanna said, lifting up her eyebrows.

"One very long night," I added.

Shanna nodded. She gave nothing away by her expression, but I had a feeling, a gut feeling, that she was impressed by what she saw.

The judges asked us a few more questions before moving onto another table.

I let out a long sigh of relief and looked at Kara.

She had a broad grin on her face.

"I think it's looking good, Cinnamon."

A feeling of relief swept through me. My muscles suddenly de-tensed. The nerves that had been shooting off like a series of bottle rockets while watching the judges make their rounds relaxed.

I gave Kara a hug.

"Thanks for being my wingman," I said. "I know it wasn't easy."

I pulled away, and her eyes were glassy like she might start crying with joy.

"I think we did it. I don't know how, but we did. We're going to Maui. I just feel it."

I smiled. I hoped she was right.

I suddenly felt those eyes on me again, and I glanced back over.

Evan was still staring at me. When he saw me look over, he nodded his head, signaling for me to come over.

Kara followed my stare.

"What's he want to talk to you for?" she asked.

"Probably about Bailey and that rock on her finger," I said.

I looked over at the judges. They still had quite a few tables to go through before they decided the winners. I had time to talk to Evan before then.

It was best to just get it out of the way. I knew that Evan was stubborn. When he wanted something, he wasn't going to quit easily.

Now was as good a time as any.

"I'll be back," I said.

"Don't do it, Cin," she said. "He shouldn't get to talk to you. He's got no right anymore."

"It's okay," I said. "Really. I'm in a good place with it now. Just give us a moment."

I left the table, and made my way over to him.

My heart was beating hard in my chest.

It was going to be hard facing the man that had destroyed so many of my dreams.

CHAPTER 39

I t was too noisy in the auditorium, so we had gone to
the front entrance to talk.

He seemed to be nervous. More nervous than me.
He kept running his hands through his hair and making
stupid small talk about the weather and the Christmas
parade and how he'd been swamped with work up at the
lodge.

It was unlike him.

But maybe in the same way it was hard for me to face
him, maybe it was hard for him to face me, knowing that
he'd ruined so many of my dreams.

Maybe it was the guilt talking.

"Hey, thanks for taking the time," he said after he
finished telling me about his job.

I didn't respond. I just stared up at him, waiting for him
to say what he'd pulled me out here to say.

I wanted him to get to the point. I already knew what he
wanted to tell me, anyway.

"So how did the judging go?" he asked.

I shrugged.

"Good, I think," I said. "But you don't really care about

that, do you? Why don't you just tell me what you're here to tell me. Get it over with already."

He was about to say something, and then he stopped. He was struggling for words.

I thought I would move things along.

"I know that you asked Bailey to marry you, okay?" I said. "And... and I wish you all the best of luck. I really do, Evan."

A confused look suddenly took hold of his face.

"What?" he said.

"I'm happy for the two of you," I said. "But don't expect me to go to your wedding or anything. Let's just leave it at that, okay? I need to get back out there. Kara's gonna be wondering where I am."

I started to leave, and then he grabbed my arm and stopped me.

"Look, I don't know what Bailey told you," he said. "But I never proposed to her. We're not engaged. Hell, that's just crazy."

"What?" I said.

He sighed.

"I think she was just trying to get in your head," Evan said.

"I can't believe she'd do that," I said.

But of course, I could. I could imagine her doing that very clearly.

I noticed that he hadn't let go of my arm.

"That's so—"

"Listen, Cin, hon," he said, pulling me off to one side of the entry hall, an area that was more private. "I'm not getting married to her. I couldn't imagine getting married again."

"I just can't believe she'd do that. I mean, that's psycho, right? Isn't that psycho? Who does that?"

"I can't blame her," he said. "I've been... I've been sort of not there for her lately. My mind's been somewhere else. You know what I mean?"

He stepped closer to me.

"No," I said. "I don't know what you mean."

"She's plum mad jealous of you," he whispered softly. "And with good reason."

He ran a finger up and down the bare skin of my lower arm. I broke out in goose bumps.

"I'm a fool, Cinnamon," he said. "I've been doing a lot of thinking. A lot of regretting. I didn't realize how good we had it. Maybe I was going through some sort of mental crisis or something. But I'm ashamed to think of how I acted and what I put you through."

"Is this an apology?" I asked.

He nodded.

"Yeah. An apology. And... Cinnamon, I miss you. My life's gone to hell since you've been gone."

I felt my legs go weak. I felt like I'd just been bitten by a swarm of mosquitoes, leaving me completely numb.

These were the words I'd been wanting to hear for two years. The ones I was certain he was going to say, but never did. The words that I dreamed about.

For him to come to his senses and realize what a giant mistake he'd made. For him to see just how badly he'd screwed up.

But now, as I heard those words, they didn't sound sweet like the way they sounded to me in the dream.

They sounded nauseating. Revolting. Sickening.

"Don't say—"

But I didn't get the words out. He suddenly scooped me up in his arms and brought his lips down to mine, and kissed me.

A kiss full of regret and desperation.

This kiss, too, I'd dreamed about for two years.

But now that my dream had come true, I didn't want it anymore.

Because as he pressed his lips on mine, those familiar smooth lips, I realized that I no longer wanted them anymore.

Without me knowing it, my dream had changed.

And Evan no longer had any part in it.

I pushed him away. But suddenly I realized, as I looked over his shoulder, that I hadn't pushed him aside in time.

My heart jumped and got caught in my throat.

Daniel was standing there in the auditorium entry way, looking at us.

It wasn't so much hurt on his face, as it was disappointment.

I pushed Evan away from me. His mouth was hanging open a little bit in surprise. He turned around to see what had caused me to react that way.

"Well," Evan said. "Am I wrong, or am I seeing a ghost?"

Daniel looked from me to him for a moment, recognizing Evan.

"Not a ghost anymore," Daniel said.

"Damn," Evan said. "Daniel Brightman. Where've you been all these years, boy?"

Daniel gave him a cautious look.

"California," he said.

"Sounds nice," Evan said. "Listen, I'd love to catch up, but I've got a few more things to talk to my wife about."

"Ex-wife," I said, glaring at him.

"Well, nonetheless," Evan said, trying to take my arm again.

I shook it free.

Huckleberry, who I suddenly noticed at Daniel's feet, started growling.

"I need to talk to Daniel," I told Evan in a firm voice.

He smiled.

"Sure," he said. "I'll let you cut in for a minute, Dan. But after, we'll finish our talk, okay Cin?"

I shivered with disgust.

He backed away, smiling. He winked at me before going back into the crowded auditorium.

And I felt like I wanted to scrub my mouth out with soap.

I couldn't believe I'd wasted so much time crying over that man.

CHAPTER 40

"Cinnamon, there's something I need to tell you. And I think you should hear it from—"

"That wasn't what it looked like," I said, nervously. "He's not... we're not—"

"We'll get to that later," Daniel said, taking his hat off.

He looked so ridiculously good and wholesome and right. Everything I'd been looking for my entire life, but clearly hadn't ever found.

Not in Evan, anyway.

I'd been bumping into furniture in the dark for years. It took a good man like Daniel to point that out to me, and a creep like Evan to really hit it home.

I saw it all now, in Technicolor.

Now I was petrified that I'd ruined any chance with Daniel. That kiss, that stupid kiss. Why hadn't I stopped Evan before it started? Why hadn't I come to my senses earlier?

What Daniel must have thought when he walked in and saw that.

I wished with all my being I could have turned the clock back five minutes. Only five minutes. And stopped it all from happening.

"First, I'm sorry I haven't called you," Daniel said.

That was funny. He was apologizing to me. It should have been the other way around.

"I drove to Portland yesterday," he said. "That's why I didn't come over yesterday."

"Portland?" I said. "Why?"

He rubbed the stubble on his chin.

"You know that knife they found on your porch?" he asked.

"Yeah?" I said, a sick feeling settling in my stomach.

Somehow, I knew what he was going to say.

It was something I'd been thinking over while frantically constructing our gingerbread house the night before.

The knife. It hadn't made sense for the burglar to leave it behind like that. It hadn't so much been left behind as planted.

Planted with evil intentions, no doubt.

Evil intentions that might just get me wrongfully accused of murder.

Someone was playing dirty. Someone was out to get me.

And destroying my gingerbread house was only the beginning.

"We think it was used in the murder," Daniel said. "Blood residue was found on the knife. A lot of blood, it looks like."

"Oh my God," I said.

The room had started spinning.

The knife. Someone had put it on my porch.

Someone was trying to frame me for Mason's murder.

Oh my God.

"But I didn't trust these yahoos with doing it right," Daniel said. "So I went to Portland, to have them process it there."

I swallowed hard.

"And?"

"They're still working on it," he said. "But there's definitely blood on that knife. We don't know who's yet but... it's not looking good."

He looked at me and for the first time, I noticed he was worried.

"Someone's trying to frame me," I said, my heart thumping away

"That's not what the Sheriff thinks," Daniel said.

"Yeah," I said, letting out a nervous sigh. "I kind of got that impression."

"I thought if I went to Portland, they could find a fingerprint or something useful that would show you didn't do it. But they didn't find anything that easy, and it's going to take a few days for more comprehensive results. And in the meantime..."

"You went all that way for me?" I asked. "The mountain pass must have been a nightmare."

"You're right," he said. "It wasn't pretty, but like I said, I don't trust these yahoos. Not enough experience with murder cases."

"But you still didn't have to do that," I said.

"Well, at the time it seemed like I did need to do that," he said.

I looked sheepishly down at the ground.

At the time.

"So what does this all mean, Daniel?" I finally said, after a few moments of silence.

He didn't say anything.

"And when they do process that knife—what good is that going to do anyway?" I said.

"There could be something the killer left behind."

I shook my head.

"I thought that was the point of planting something," I said. "To frame someone. Not to implicate yourself."

"But this wasn't some cold-blooded murder," Daniel said. "I think Mason knew whoever killed him, and I think he knew them well. There are emotions involved. That makes whoever did this open to sloppiness."

"I can't believe this is happening," I said. "I can't believe that anyone would believe that I did this. That I could be capable of killing over some cookies and frosting."

"That's just Sheriff Trumbow who thinks that," Daniel said, looking away from me. "I know you didn't do it. For whatever that's worth."

That same disappointed look was on his face, and I felt rotten, not so much because I was about to be accused of murder, but because I knew that on some level, I had hurt him.

"It's worth a lot," I said, reaching for his hand. "It means the world."

He didn't look at me, and I knew I hadn't gotten through to him.

If he could just hear me out. If I could just explain it, if he just understood what I had gone through for the past two years and what I had learned in the past of 48 hours.

But I wouldn't get my chance to tell him.

"You should get back in there," he said. "I've got a few things to do, too."

"Daniel, I—"

"It's okay," he said. "We'll talk later."

He walked away from me, into the packed auditorium. I wanted to chase after him, tell him to stop, to listen to me, that nothing was more important than he hear me out on this. That what I felt for him was more important than the bloody knife or someone trying to frame me or broken gingerbread houses or winning stupid competitions.

But I couldn't seem to make my feet move after him. I stood, stunned, trapped in some sort of web I couldn't get out of. Just gazing at the empty hallway where he had been.

CHAPTER 41

The crowd was starting to get antsy.

The judges had been conversing now for half an hour and it appeared that they still hadn't chosen a winner yet.

I felt the knot in my stomach tighten. I watched Bailey from across the room. Evan was standing beside her. They looked like a happy couple. Like he hadn't just kissed me in the hallway.

It made me want to vomit, realizing that where Bailey was now, I was two years ago. Evan and I had looked like the perfect couple. He was good at that. Good at being one half of the perfect couple. Even when he was cheating on the other half.

I looked at him with disgust. How foolish I had been.

I searched the crowd, looking for Daniel, for his trademark cowboy hat, for that tall, graceful figure, but I didn't see him anywhere.

I sighed.

I wondered if I should find Sheriff Trumbow and tell him about Bailey and the evidence of her sabotage.

But then I remembered how he treated me the last time I brought Bailey up.

With suspicion. Like I was the jealous ex-wife who wanted to frame her.

Frame *her*. That was funny.

"What are they talking about already?" Kara said, shaking out her arms out nervously. "There's nothing to discuss. Ours is the best."

I tried to smile, but had a tough time doing it.

I just wanted the judges to come out and announce the winner. I didn't even care if it was us anymore.

I just needed to get this over so I could talk to Daniel.

I couldn't focus on anything else.

"Hey, you still alive there, Cin?" Kara asked, waving a hand in front of my face.

I shook my head.

"I'm just tired," I lied. "I just want this to be over."

"I know what you mean," Kara said. "When this is all over I'm going to take a giant na—"

"Cinnamon Peters," a deep voice said from behind me.

The voice was familiar.

I turned around, my heart dropping floor after floor, down, down, down as I realized what was going on.

Sheriff Trumbow was standing in front of me, an authoritative look on his face. To my right, a camera with an eager-looking reporter was leering at me.

My mouth suddenly went as dry as the high deserts of Eastern Oregon.

I couldn't say anything.

All I could think was:

Sheriff Trumbow, you son of a…

"Cinnamon Peters, you're under arrest for the murder of Mason Barstow."

I gripped the table, and looked around at all the eyes staring at me.

None of it had seemed real until this moment. Mason's death, the break-in, the knife on the porch.

But now, now, it was more real than I could possibly have imagined.

As real as the cold steel bars of a jail cell.

CHAPTER 42

The sheriff had grabbed my wrists and started placing metal cuffs on them when a scream ripped through the crowd.

It was a scream of pain, of agony, of frantic hurt.

"Get this damned animal off me!" a woman screamed. "Get it off me!"

Sheriff Trumbow loosened his grip on my wrists. The news reporter and her camera man stood on their tiptoes, trying to see over the crowd of people.

There were too many people in the crowd to see what was going on.

Sheriff Trumbow looked at me sternly.

"Don't you go anywhere," he said.

He let go of my wrists and started pushing his way through the crowd, his big frame bumping people left and right.

"Move it, folks," he said. "Make way!"

For the most part they didn't listen to him, and he had to fight his way through.

"Get Mason's damn runt away from me!" the voice cried again.

There was something familiar in the voice. But in the high-pitched shrieks, I had trouble placing it.

I watched as the sheriff got knocked aside by a tourist who had accidently backed up into him. He was useless.

I disobeyed the sheriff. I left where I was standing and went away from the crowd, sweeping around, threading through the masses until the cries became louder and louder. I pushed my way through, finally making it to the huddle of people surrounding whoever was being attacked.

I saw the familiar cowboy hat, and squeezed through.

Daniel was looking down at the woman on the ground.

I followed his gaze.

And my mouth fell open.

CHAPTER 43

Huckleberry had a hold of Gretchen O'Malley's leg like it was a drumstick that someone had used to beat him with, and he was getting his revenge.

He let out a low guttural growl and held his jaw firmly clamped on her calf. He shook it, and she screamed again, her cries echoing through the gymnasium.

The strange thing was, though, that nobody was doing anything. It was as if we were stuck in a snow globe, watching the scene unfold in a glass orb of water.

Daniel had the leash wrapped around his hand, but he wasn't tightening it. He was just staring down at Gretchen, a look of perfect understanding on his face.

"Will someone please help that woman!" Sheriff Trumbow shouted from somewhere back in the crowd.

"Yes, please help!" she shouted.

Huckleberry shook her leg again and she let out another cry.

Daniel suddenly kneeled down beside her.

"You killed him, didn't you?" Daniel said. "You killed Mason Barstow."

"I… I don't know what you're talking about!" she cried,

her face red and puffy, her hair a tangled mess.

"You do, I know you do. The dog knows you did it and so do I. Say it."

She tried to lash out at Huckleberry, but he came back at her tenfold.

She screamed again. It was bordering on torture, now. I placed a hand on Daniel's shoulder, but he didn't seem to notice.

"She's bleeding, Danie—"

"Fine!" she cried. "I did it! But I didn't mean to. I didn't mean to do it. I swear!"

Daniel pulled back on the leash, and Huckleberry was yanked backwards. He continued to growl though, a look of insane vengeance in his eyes.

I knew at that moment, seeing the anger in little Huck's eyes, that it was true.

The dog didn't lie.

Gretchen had killed Mason. And Huckleberry had seen it happen.

And now he was avenging his dead master.

Gretchen moaned in pain, and finally Sheriff Trumbow appeared, red in the face and out of breath.

"Someone call this woman an ambulance!" he cried out. "And you get that mutt out of here, Brightman!"

Sheriff Trumbow saw me, and then pushed his way over to me.

"Cinnamon Peters, you're under arrest for the murder of—"

"No," Daniel said, standing up from his position

kneeling over Gretchen. "This is who you want here, Sheriff."

He stood in front of me, protecting me, and then nodded to Gretchen, who was whimpering in a fetal position on the cold auditorium floor.

"This is your killer," he said, nodding to her.

CHAPTER 44

There was no trip to Hawaii for Kara or me.

There was no trip to Hawaii for Gretchen either. Or Bailey for that matter.

Nobody got the grand prize. Because after the freak show that had taken place at the competition, after Christmas River showed up on every news station radar for 500 miles around, the annual Gingerbread Junction Competition was cancelled for the first time since anyone could remember.

The organizers came out with a statement saying they were wrong in letting it continue after Mason was found murdered under suspicious circumstances. They said their actions had been unbecoming of such a prestigious competition. One of the organizers stepped down, and there were promises of regulating next year's competition so it wouldn't ever get out of hand again.

There was a lot of national media attention. A lot of stories about Gretchen and Mason, and how the murder unfolded. Some of them even mentioned me and how I found the body behind my shop, and that Gretchen had tried to frame me, her gingerbread junction archenemy.

I couldn't complain with the publicity, though. It

brought a flood of tourists to my shop. Tourists who came in to get the gory details of the murder and left with a full stomach of homemade pie. Tourists who left behind generous tips.

It wasn't even Christmas yet, and I had already doubled my earnings from the December before.

The details of the murder eventually came out, though I heard it mostly from second hand sources.

Even after everything I had seen, I still had trouble believing it all.

Nobody knew exactly how long the affair had gone on for. It could have been years, or just a few months. The first record of it was a credit card receipt from the High Springs Lodge four months earlier. Gretchen had bought dinner for two there. Mason, a room. Both were on the same night.

It was hard for me to imagine… the two of them. They were both so old, so past the reasonable age to do something like that, if there ever was a reasonable age to do something like that.

From there, though, it appeared that things went south. In a search of Gretchen's house, they found a note stuffed inside the base of a lamp on her nightstand that was written by Mason.

Promises had been made, and promises appeared to have been broken. Mason was going to tell Gretchen's husband about the affair.

Apparently, it never got to that point, though.

One thing I wondered a lot after all the details came out was whether or not Gretchen had gone on a walk with him that day planning to kill him. She'd brought the knife along. That showed premeditation of some sort.

But maybe she only wanted to threaten him, or get him to listen or get him to leave her alone.

But either way, the story ended the same. With Mason dead in the woods, a knife wound in his chest, the snow around him red with his blood.

But there was one thing Gretchen hadn't counted on.

She hadn't counted on Huckleberry.

She must have just expected him to run away, but he didn't.

He attacked her. Police found partially healed bite wounds on her calf, the same one he later grabbed a hold of at the competition.

She broke free, though, made it out of the woods, and got in her car, leaving it all behind.

But then she realized that in all the terror and excitement of the moment, she'd forgotten one thing.

The knife.

She'd left the knife behind. Without knowing if they'd be able to trace it back to her somehow.

The police thought that she probably took some time to think about her next move, and finally settled on the wild notion of framing me for the murder. Our gingerbread rivalry was well-documented, and police believe she looked at it as killing two birds with one stone.

At some point, she left the knife on my back porch, sometime after she got word that Mason's body was found.

The police said that she also broke into my shop to draw

attention and move the process along a little bit, but they had no real proof on that end.

And besides. I knew better on that one.

That particular instance of breaking the law still had Bailey's name written all over it.

But since there was no evidence to support what I knew, there was no way I could press charges.

And besides, even if there was, I didn't know if I would have pressed them. I had already gotten back at Bailey. And my form of revenge had been way better than breaking a window and reducing a gingerbread house to a pile of rubble.

Gretchen was now in police custody, charged with murder in the first degree pending an official trial date.

When I thought about it, part of me couldn't help but feel sorry for Gretchen O'Malley. I didn't know why. She'd tried to frame me for murder, and if it hadn't been for Huckleberry, I'd be the one sitting in that cold jail cell.

But I thought back to that day she'd come into my shop, right before the competition. And looking back, I now realized what I saw was an unsure woman, not necessarily a malicious one. She'd done something bad, and she knew it. And she'd come into my shop that day with a guilty conscience.

I'd disliked Gretchen since the very moment I'd met her nearly two decades ago. She represented the opposite of what I wanted to be. She was snobby, cold, and harsh.

But she was human, too. Just like any of us, she'd gotten caught up in a web of love, lies, and deceit. It got to the point where she couldn't see straight anymore, and she lost her way. The same as getting caught out in a blizzard. She'd lost all sense of direction.

So much so that she felt she had to resort to murder to free herself from it.

There were parts of her story I could relate to. Parts of it that I knew could have easily been me, in another lifetime.

I felt sorry for her. And her story, her fall, had given me some much-needed perspective.

Winning wasn't everything. Trips to Hawaii were nice, but in the big scheme of things, Hawaii was just a place on the map.

There were more important things.

More important things I had to take care of.

CHAPTER 45

We met on the wooden footbridge to talk.

I called him several times and sent text messages and even stopped by his house, but heard nothing for days.

Then, out of the blue, he responded to one of my text messages. He wanted to meet.

I couldn't get out of the shop until late. The sun was on the horizon by the time we got to the footbridge, and the whole world seemed to turn an ominous shade of red as the day died.

I was nervous. It felt like a handful of rocks were in my stomach, bumping into one another as I walked.

I pulled my down jacket tighter around my body.

I saw him from a distance. He was leaning over the wooden railing, looking down at the frozen river.

"We used to fish off this bridge, my brother and me when we were kids," he said as I came up to him. "We used to come home with a string full of trout."

"Listen, Daniel," I said, my voice shaking. "Thanks for everything you did. For saving me. I'm pretty sure I'd be behind bars right now if it wasn't for you."

Daniel shook his head.

"They would have figured it out eventually," he said. "But how long it would have taken, I don't know. The sheriff's not the brightest color in the crayon box."

I forced a smile.

"No he isn't."

"It sounds like this might ruin his chances for reelection," Daniel said. "The whole country saw his IQ level with this case."

"Well, it'd be good to get some fresh blood around here," I said, feeling more and more like we were just making meaningless small talk to replace the things that we really wanted to say. "It's always good not to let things get too stale."

He nodded and didn't say anything more.

I took a deep breath and let out everything I'd wanted to say to him since that day at the Gingerbread Junction.

"What you saw the other day, between me and Evan? It didn't mean anything, Daniel. I don't love Evan. I don't even like him. He's a bad person. It's taken me all this time to realize it, but he's a really bad person. I don't want someone like that in my life. I want someone like…"

I trailed off. I couldn't finish the thought for some reason.

There was an awkward silence where he left me hanging like I was one of those trout on his fishing line. We both looked out at the frozen river. A group of ducks were sliding across the ice.

"Do you know why I came back home to Christmas

River? Why I really came back home?" he asked.

I looked over at him and shook my head.

"Seventeen years ago I went to California to become a cop and look for my brother's killer," he said, leaning against the railing. "It was a convenience store robbery, and the guy who did it was never caught. Nobody cared about the case. Only I cared."

"Did you ever find him?" I asked.

He nodded his head somberly.

"It took a decade and a half, but I did it. I tracked the bastard down."

He stopped talking for a moment. The last of the blood-red color drained from the sky, giving way to a dead gray shade.

"What hap—"

"I always thought when the moment came, I'd know exactly what to do," he said, not meeting my gaze. "I thought I'd be able to control myself. But I was wrong."

I gripped the railing.

This whole time, I'd sensed there was more to the reason why he was back in Christmas River, and now, it was beginning to make more sense.

"Did you kill him?" I asked, my voice barely above a whisper.

He shook his head.

"No," he said. "But I hurt him. I hurt him pretty bad. The department covered for me, even though they shouldn't have. Anybody else would've gotten their badge taken away."

He sighed.

"But I couldn't do it anymore. I couldn't pretend to be a police officer, a protector, after what I did. And there's not a day that goes by that I don't think of what I did to that guy. The way he looked after I got through with him."

I looked over at him. His face was wracked with guilt.

"I'm sure he deserved it," I said. "He murdered your brother."

Daniel shook his head.

"Before, I would have agreed with you," he said. "But not anymore. I saw a part of myself... I can't ever accept that part. It was evil. Just pure hate."

"We all have that in us. That doesn't make you evil."

He put his hat back on.

"That's not an excuse," he said. "I violated everything I believed in that day. I'm worthless now."

"I don't believe that," I said. "For whatever it's worth."

"I thought it would help to come back home," he said. "To get out in the woods and try and forget about it all. But nothing helps. I still wake up thinking about what I did."

He stuffed his hands in his pockets and started backing away from me.

"I can't stay here any longer," he said. "It's no good. Nowhere is."

"Wait," I said, stepping forward, picking up the space he had created between us. "You can't—"

"Goodbye, Cinnamon," he said. "I'm sorry if I've hurt you. I'm sorry for everything I've done to you. See what I mean? See how I'm doing this to you all over again? I'm worthless."

He turned his back on me and walked away quickly. The bridge shook under his boots.

"Wait," I whispered.

But he didn't hear me. He disappeared into the trees as the footpath continued into the woods.

He was walking out of my life, once again.

CHAPTER 46

I was working on a batch of cherry pies when I heard the front door jingle.

I wiped my hands on my apron, and yelled that I would be right there as I shoved a panful of the filled pies into the oven.

It had been a relatively quiet morning. A welcome relief after the flurry of tourists looking for macabre stories of the murder.

I had even gotten to sit down with a cup of coffee at one point and read a baking magazine, something I hadn't done in what seemed like weeks.

But it was approaching Christmas, and the tourists were starting to return home for the holiday. There'd be another wave of them for New Year's, but we were just beginning to settle into the eye of the hurricane.

I wiped my face free of flour marks, and emerged from the kitchen into the cozy dining room.

In the back of my mind, I secretly hoped it was him.

I hoped, hope against hope, that he'd changed his mind. That Daniel would stay. That he wouldn't leave me and Christmas River forever in his rearview mirror.

But maybe it was for the best. Maybe when a moment passes, you can't ever reclaim it. Maybe it's best to leave that white hot love of youth behind in the dirt where you left it, because nobody ever remains the same. Life changes us. And the two teenagers who kissed under that moonlit night on the lake all those years ago were gone. They didn't exist anymore. All that was left were two adults who brought with them endless amounts of baggage and hurts and pains.

Maybe it was just never meant to be.

That was what I wanted to believe anyway.

The truth, of course, was that I didn't believe it.

Daniel had left me heartbroken, yet again.

I went to the cash register.

"The usual, if you would," John said, taking off his scarf and coat.

"Well hey there, stranger," I said, smiling. "Long time no, see. I've got a backlog of strawberry rhubarbs nobody's touched for a week."

He smiled back. A real smile. Not the usual nervous one he gave me.

"Yeah," he said. "Sorry. I left town for a week. Went to go visit my folks and clear my head a little bit. I didn't get a chance to tell you with everything going on."

I sliced a big piece of the pie for him, and placed it on the plate.

"I hope your folks are doing well," I said.

"Yeah. I mean, loud and brash, but that's normal for them."

I smiled. I always got the impression that John's family embarrassed him on some levels.

"Listen," he said. "There's something I came over to talk to you ab—"

Just as he said that, a gust of cold air blew through the shop as the front door opened. The door jingle bell slapped back and forth across the glass.

My stomach tightened as he walked in, tracking snow into the dining room.

"You're so popular these days," he said. "So much competition I've got."

A groan of disappointment escaped my mouth, which was followed by an awkward silence.

"Aw, don't tell me you're not glad to see me, Cin," he said.

"What do you want, Evan?" I said, trying to keep my voice steady.

"To finish that conversation we started the other day."

He suddenly looked at John.

"Would you leave us for a moment? Cinnamon and I have a few things to discuss."

John didn't say anything. But he stayed where he was. He wasn't about to back down.

Evan approached the counter, leaning over. He started saying things in a low, honeyed voice.

"It's finished, Cinnamon," he said. "I told Bailey that I didn't want her anymore."

I cleared my throat, adjusting my stance.

"That's great," I said. "What does that have to do with me?"

He smiled. An almost-cruel smile that sent my skin crawling.

"Everything, honey," he said. "I meant what I said that day. That I can't live without you. That I'm sorry for what I did. I was a damn fool. I made a mistake. I just... I lost it there for a while."

"Two years," I said. "You lost it for two damn years."

He looked away and back at me.

"It's all in the past now, honey bun," he said, reaching over and stroking my hand. "We've got our whole future ahead of us, now. I'm back, Cinnamon. I'm back and I'll never do that to you again."

I bit my lip and felt my eyes welling up with tears.

I wanted to kick myself. I didn't even know why I was crying. It was just a reaction. I was overwhelmed with so much emotion, I couldn't control myself.

"Aw, see," Evan said, dipping his head so he could meet my lowered eyes. "I know you still love me. I've known it the whole time. You belong to me, Cinnamon."

You belong to me...

It was that last line that really did me in.

That last line that broke me down.

The last line that really hit it home.

I pulled my hand back like I was escaping the sharp teeth of a striking rattlesnake.

"Get out of here, Evan," I said, my voice quiet and shaky.

He looked deep into my eyes, and we both knew, in that instance, that the tables had turned.

That I was the one now who had the power.

"You don't mean that," he said.

"Get *OUT* of here," I said, raising my voice. "Or so help

me, I'll throw you out myself."

He stood up straight, looking at me with pained eyes, or whatever insincere emotion he really felt.

"It's over, Evan," I said. "It has been since the moment you stepped out on me."

He stood there for a moment, stunned.

And then he shook his head angrily.

"All the same," he said, backing away. "You're all the same. But that's okay. There's a million out there just like you who'd love to take what I'm offering."

"Then find yourself one," I said. "And leave me out of it."

He gave John a hateful look, and then opened up the front door, slamming it hard behind him. I watched him stomp across the street, like a child throwing a tantrum.

And I hoped that would be the last time I ever saw Evan.

That he was now, officially and finally, out of my life forever.

CHAPTER 47

"I'm sorry about that," I said to John when I'd regained my composure.

I sat down across from him at his booth, the uneaten slice of strawberry rhubarb between us. Something I rarely did. But because nobody was coming in, I had a little extra time.

He held up his hand.

"Don't worry about it."

"Thanks, uh, thanks for having my back there, too," I said. "It's nice to know I have someone I can count on."

"I'm glad to do it, Cinnamon," he said, poking at the pie with the prongs of his fork. "I'll always be there for you if you need me."

I nodded, and took a deep breath. I stared out the window, at the Christmas decorations lining the snow-covered streets, and then I looked back at him.

It was time to tell him. To do the right thing.

To tell him there was no chance of this ever going beyond what it was now.

"Listen, John, I'm glad you came in today," I said. "There's something I've been wanting to talk to you about."

He reached across the table, and placed his hand on mine. It was warm and gentle.

"You don't need to," he said. "I already know how you feel about me."

I raised my eyebrows.

"I've always known it, but I saw it clearly that day that Daniel guy came into the shop. I saw something in you then that I'd never seen when I've looked at you."

I sighed.

"I'm that easy to read, am I?" I said.

He shrugged.

"It's easy to read a woman when she's not in love with you."

I bit my lower lip.

"I feel like a real…" I said, struggling to find the right word to describe the poor way I had acted. "A real ass. I should have told you sooner. I didn't want you to think I was leading you on or something."

"I know," he said. "I wanted something that just wasn't working. I wanted it so badly that I couldn't even see that it wasn't working. But listen, Cinnamon, I don't mind. Really. Not anymore."

"Not anymore?" I said.

He smiled. A bashful kind of grin that I'd never seen on him.

"Well, that's why I'm here," he said. "I wanted to ask you something."

"Oh?" I said.

I couldn't possibly think of what he meant.

"I know this is kind of formal, but we both thought that it would be wrong to sneak around behind your back. But I just wanted to ask you if you'd mind if Kara and I... you know. If we started seeing each other."

My jaw nearly hit the floor.

John and Kara?

I wouldn't have put them together myself in a million years.

But once the initial shock wore off, it started making sense.

I could see the qualities that each of them would be drawn to. John was serious and down to earth. Kara was vibrant and full of energy and life.

"You see, I'd seen her a few times in your shop before," he said, his voice quaking a little. "And... well, we talked a few times and we hit it off. I just wanted to make sure that you didn't mind, though."

I was silent for a moment, processing it all.

It was still hard to believe, but the more and more I thought about it, the more... the more it seemed right, in some sort of strange way.

John stared at me intently, waiting for my reply.

I smiled.

"John, I'm not her father or anything," I said. "You don't have to ask me my permission. But I appreciate you doing it."

He let out a long sigh of relief.

"And I hope... I wish you all the happiness in the world. Truly I do," I said.

I held my hand out across the table to meet his.

"Friends?" I said.

He took it after a moment.

"Friends," he said, gripping my hand sternly.

I got up from the table.

"But I warn you," I said. "You've better start getting some new clients at your practice. Strawberry rhubarb pie's a lot cheaper than the ornaments Kara sells at her boutique."

He laughed.

"And not nearly as tasty, either," he said.

I grabbed the slice of uneaten pie from the table.

"Does this mean I can stop making this flavor for you?" I said. "You're about the only one who orders it these days."

"Well, I guess," he said. "But don't count me out completely. I'll still stop by from time to time if that's okay with you."

I smiled at him before leaving his table to go in the back and check on the cherry pies baking in the oven.

"Of course it is," I said. "My door's always open to my friends."

He got up, and tried to pay, but I wouldn't have it.

His money was no good here.

CHAPTER 48

It was Christmas Eve day, and after making a fresh batch of pies, I closed up the shop early, and went for a long walk in the woods.

It felt like I'd spent the entire month slaving away in front of a hot oven, baking pies and rolling dough and building houses that all eventually crumbled to the ground.

The sky had a cold, steely look to it, and the air smelled like snow. Christmas lights and wreaths hung from bannisters as I left downtown, and took the footbridge over the river and got to Shevlin Trail.

I dug my hands deep in my coat, and tried to think about everything I was thankful for, as I always tried to do on Christmas Eve.

I was thankful for my family. For Warren, who I could always go to for anything. For Kara, who always had my back, no matter what.

I thought about her now. She'd been as embarrassed as I'd ever seen her when I told her what John had said to me. She'd said she was going to ask me herself, as soon as everything settled down. It almost seemed as though she felt bad about it. But there was no reason to.

As long as she was happy, so was I.

And she did seem to be happy. When she talked about John, it wasn't in that same, humorous, condescending way she usually talked about men. She respected him.

It made me so happy to hear it. It had been ages since I heard her talk that way about any man.

Things seemed to have worked themselves out. John and Kara, Bailey and Evan. Everyone seemed to have gotten exactly what they deserved.

Maybe I had too.

I walked deeper into the woods, Listening to the sound of my boots crunching against a layer of old snow. Listening to the trees creak in the wind and feeling the cold wind blowing against my cheeks. Birds were whistling in the bare branches, their song filling up the forest.

I was strong, though. I would move past it. I'd had plenty of experience with broken hearts. I knew that after a little while, the noose of pain would loosen its grip around my throat. I knew that one day this would all be a distant memory. One day, I'd find someone new and learn to love again.

Until then, I would just do the best I could.

So much of life seemed to be about loss. About people coming and going out of your life. Of the empty voids they left behind when they did.

I thought about Daniel, even though I told myself not to. I thought of little Huckleberry, even though I told myself not to.

I hoped both of them were safe. Warm and safe with full hearts and stomachs.

In the end, that was all I could do. Hope.

I walked through the forest with a heavy heart until the sun started sinking low in the sky.

Then, I popped over to the Christmas River Catholic Church. The one that my mom used to take me to when I was a kid. She had a strong faith, unlike my grandfather or me.

I went inside, opening the giant doors, and I walked down the long aisle up to the altar. The church was mostly empty, save for a few volunteers readying the pews for Christmas Eve mass.

I went to the row of candles flickering on the table, and I lit one for my mom. Thinking about how much I still missed her.

After I left the church, I went back to the shop and loaded up a shopping bag full of the meat pies.

I would deliver them to the humane society after I picked Warren up from the tavern and dropped him back home. The dogs would have them for Christmas morning.

Because even dogs deserved to have a merry Christmas.

CHAPTER 49

"I've got the eggnog under control, honey," Warren said as we drove along the cold and frozen streets. "You just get yourself home before eight."

He'd had a bagful of groceries at his feet. He'd walked to the store a few blocks from our house, and I had picked him up and was dropping him back off at home.

"Okay," I said. "You fellas just pace yourself, though, okay? It's a long ways until midnight."

Warren was having a few of the boys over for some eggnog and to play some poker before watching the Vatican's Christmas Eve mass on TV.

Leave it to Warren to gamble and watch the Pope ring in Christmas all in the same night.

It was a tradition he'd had for years, though. Ever since Grandma Mae passed, he'd spent the eve before Christmas surrounded by his buddies, and me. This year, Kara was going to stop by too for a little while. But she had Christmas Eve dinner with her folks, so she wouldn't be able to stay long.

I pulled up to the house and Warren got out.

"Hey, one thing," he said, leaning into the car. "I've got

one more guest on the list tonight, if you don't mind."

"Oh yeah?" I said, raising my eyebrow.

I'd thought that he'd already invited all his friends from the tavern, but maybe he'd missed someone.

"Yeah," he said, hesitantly. "Her name… it's Catherine."

"Oh?" I said. "Catherine Harris? The new barmaid at the Pine?"

Catherine was new to town, in her mid-60s, and worked at the tavern on the weekends to supplement her social security checks. She was a widow whose husband had died about ten years earlier.

"I think she prefers the term *bartender*," Warren said.

"Oh… so it's like that, is it?"

Warren's face broke out into a giant smile.

"If I'm lucky," he said.

"That makes me real happy," I said. "I look forward to seeing her later."

I laughed at that big grin on his face.

"You old dog," I said. "Get out of here already."

"Okay, but you hurry home now," he said, winking at me.

He was laughing as he shut the car door and walked up the steps to the house.

I watched, making sure he was safely in. Then, I drove back over to the shop.

The streets were deserted. As deserted as they ever got in Christmas River. It was ironic. The night before the biggest holiday, and Christmas River felt like a ghost town.

The lights were on everywhere, but the shops were dark.

Soft snow was starting to come down from the sky, but it wasn't magical. It was bleak and cold and empty.

I sighed, and got out. I went in the shop and grabbed the bag of meat pies, and walked a few blocks to the humane society.

The lights were on, but the door was locked. I knocked on it several times, but nobody answered.

"Damn it," I muttered out loud.

I knew someone was in there caring for the dogs, but they didn't seem to want to answer the door.

I sighed, the shopping bag of pies feeling heavy in my hands.

Finally, I set it down on the doorstep and walked away down the icy steps.

The dogs would eventually get the pies.

But it didn't leave me with that warm and cozy feeling I'd been searching for. That feeling of doing something good for someone, or something.

It left me feeling cold and empty, like a hollow chocolate Santa.

I walked slowly back to the shop, through the thick falling snow, not caring that I was getting drenched.

CHAPTER 50

I walked into the shop, not bothering to stomp off the snow that had collected on my boots.

I took my jacket and scarf off, and hung them up on the coat rack.

There was still a load of dishes left to do before I could close up. I thought for a moment about just leaving them until the day after Christmas, but knew that they'd be even more a pain to do then.

I stood over the sink, scrubbing out bowls and utensils, and placing them in the dishwasher.

It was no good, though. Doing dishes just led to my thoughts wandering all over the place.

And that, inevitably, led to regret.

I felt the lump growing in my throat and my eyes starting to grow heavy and waterlogged.

I wanted to pretend it was just the steam from the hot water causing it to happen, but who was I kidding? There was no one left to kid. Just me, alone, scrubbing dishes on Christmas, miserable and alone, and probably having years and years of the same scenario to look forward to.

I wasn't sentimental. I wasn't sappy or soft or gooey.

But I was human.

And I was sad. And lonely. A kind of loneliness that all the spiked eggnog in the world wouldn't make go away.

I placed a handful of forks and knives in the dishwasher, and shut it. I took off my apron, and sighed, glancing at my reflection in the dark window pane.

Another Christmas. And soon another year.

And soon, 34.

And every year here on out, it would just get wors—

Suddenly, there was a loud noise from the back porch.

The sound of something scratching at the window pane.

My heart jumped in my throat.

I placed my face up to the window, and cupped my hands around my head to see past the reflection.

I looked down.

And that's when I saw him.

He was healthy and happy-looking. His fur, which had once been matted and dirty, was now shiny and smooth. The tear stains from around his eyes were gone. He no longer had that look of hunger in his little brown eyes.

And he was at the sliding glass door, bringing his paw up to the window, and scratching at it.

My heart suddenly broke free of the basement it'd been stored in since that night we had kissed under the winter moonlight.

And it soared, breaking through walls and ceilings as it ascended higher and higher.

I opened the door. Huckleberry came rushing in. I kneeled down and he started licking my face and whimpering, as if greeting an old friend.

I wrapped my arms around him, holding onto his silky fur and kissing his sweet soft head.

"I've missed you so much, Hucks."

He nuzzled me behind my ear, tickling me. I started laughing.

Finally, after a few moments, I stood up, and stepped outside. It was snowing hard now, big flakes of snow coming down from the red sky, blanketing the trees with a fresh white coating.

I couldn't see anything, but suddenly, over the breeze and the swaying of the trees, I heard something.

Music.

A soft sound at first. Quiet and distant.

The strumming of guitar strings. Then a voice. Hushed at first, but then it started rising.

Louder and louder, I squinted in the snow storm, looking at the silhouette coming toward me. The wind carrying the song to me.

I bit my lip, trying to hold back the tears as the figure stepped into the warm glow cast by the kitchen light.

It was him.

I couldn't believe it. For a moment, I just stared at him, stunned.

He was wearing his buffalo plaid jacket, The same one he'd come to my porch that night in, chasing after Huckleberry. He wasn't wearing his hat, and flakes were gathering in his dark hair. The soft glow of the kitchen light fell on his face, illuminating it, making him look like an angel troubadour, descended from heaven to save my broken heart.

His eyes reached for mine. He smiled. A smile filled with everything I'd been missing in my life these past few years. Hell, these past 16 years. Ever since that night standing at the banks of the lake, when he made me feel like I was the most important person in the world.

A tear slid down my face, and I knew I was cooked.

I was.

I was sentimental. I was sappy. I was soft and gooey.

The walls came crashing down around me.

He turned all my hard edges into soft ones. All my cynicism into optimism. All my despair into hope.

Daniel Brightman, singing an Otis Redding song about how strong his love was on a snowy Christmas Eve on the back porch of my shop, ruined the cold, empty person that I had been.

He came to the end of the song, and my face was melted with tears.

"Cinnamon," he said, putting down the guitar. "If I could take back these past 16 years, I would. I would go back to that lake with you, and never want anything else."

He took my hand in his, and stared down at me. I fell deeper and deeper into those green eyes.

"But I can't do that," he said. "All I can offer you is what I am today. My heart, damaged as it is. And a promise to never leave you ever again."

I was speechless.

I realized these were the words I'd always wanted to hear. My entire life.

I knew I should have been mad. Mad that he'd left and abandoned me again. The old me would have been. The one who'd been beaten up and changed by harsh realities of life.

But when I was with Daniel, I felt like that 16-year-old, under the moonlight, listening to him sing. Fresh and clean and unscathed by the bitter side of love. Complete.

"Don't do that to me again," I said, placing a hand up to his cheek. "Ever."

"I couldn't," he said, touching my hand. "I love you too much."

He wrapped his arms around me and pulled me close, and we kissed, the snow falling silently all around us, the wind blowing sharply into the sides of our faces.

But I wasn't cold. In fact, I hadn't been that warm in years.

Huckleberry circled us, wagging his little nub, barking playfully.

Daniel kissed me like he did that night in the summer of our youth. Deep and passionate and soul-shaking.

And I knew he was true. I knew he was never going to leave me. Not ever again.

EPILOGUE

The dog has never tasted anything as delicious as this meat pie the woman had placed for him in the corner of her kitchen.

He ate at it noisily, some of it splashing over the sides. It felt good to be inside, to be warm, to feel that he was loved and wanted again.

Soft music played from the speakers and the man held the woman, and they swayed gently from side to side to the rhythm.

And the dog had a feeling that he'd be seeing a lot more of the woman.

That the man and the woman would play a big part in his life in the upcoming years.

He would be loyal to both of them and would never leave their sides as long as he lived.

Huckleberry, as the woman called him, finally had a loving home.

He was no longer alone.

Don't miss out on great deals on Meg's books! Sign up for Meg Muldoon's mailing list by visiting www.megmuldoon.com, and in addition to monthly newsletters, you'll also get a recipe booklet and a free digital copy of *Roasted in Christmas River: A Thanksgiving Cozy Mystery Novella*!

And for more cozy fun, join Meg on Facebook, Instagram, and Goodreads.

The Christmas River Cozy Mystery Collection

Murder in Christmas River (Book 1)
Mayhem in Christmas River (Book 2)
Madness in Christmas River (Book 3)
Malice in Christmas River (Book 4)
Mischief in Christmas River (Book 5)
Manic in Christmas River (Book 6)
Magic in Christmas River (Book 7)
Menace in Christmas River (Book 8)
Missing in Christmas River (Book 9)
Meltdown in Christmas River (Book 10)
Midnight in Christmas River (Book 11)
Mistake in Christmas River (Book 12)
Roasted in Christmas River (Novella)

ABOUT THE AUTHOR

Bestselling author Meg Muldoon loves writing cozy mysteries. A former small town news reporter, Meg has always had a special place in her heart for lost dogs, homeless cats, and feisty old locals. She enjoys bourbon bread pudding, red cowboy boots and craft glue guns.

Originally from Central Oregon, Meg lives in Arizona with two Great Pyrenees and a cattle dog named Huckleberry.

For more about Meg and her other cozy mystery series, visit her website www.megmuldoon.com.

Made in United States
North Haven, CT
09 December 2024

62048306R00133